"Johnny, Don't Kiss Me."

Before he could misunderstand, Francesca rushed on. "I want you to kiss me, but don't, because if you do, I'm gonna do something crazy, and I can't do anything crazy because I have to go to work."

He did draw back, but the look he gave her left her as feverish as he'd been. "Maybe you should throw me out of here. I can't seem to resist touching you."

"Maybe that's why I can't throw you out, Johnny. No one's ever found it a problem to resist me before."

"Ah, sweetheart…" He took hold of her hand and placed an ardent kiss in her palm. "Don't tell me things like that. It puts even crazier ideas in my head than are already there."

Dear Reader,

Welcome to the wonderful world of Silhouette Desire! This month, look for six scintillating love stories. I know you're going to enjoy them all. First up is *The Beauty, the Beast and the Baby*, a fabulous MAN OF THE MONTH from Dixie Browning. It's also the second book in her TALL, DARK AND HANDSOME miniseries.

The exciting SONS AND LOVERS series also continues with Leanne Banks's *Ridge: The Avenger*. This is Leanne's first Silhouette Desire, but she certainly isn't new to writing romance.

This month, Desire has *Husband: Optional*, the next installment of Marie Ferrarella's THE BABY OF THE MONTH CLUB. Don't worry if you've missed earlier titles in this series, because this book "stands alone." And it's so charming and breezy you're sure to just love it!

The WEDDING BELLES series by Carole Buck is completed with *Zoe and the Best Man*. This series just keeps getting better and better, and Gabriel Flynn is one scrumptious hero.

Next is Kristin James' Desire, *The Last Groom on Earth*, a delicious opposites-attract story written with Kristin's trademark sensuality.

Rounding out the month is an amnesia story (one of my *favorite* story twists), *Just a Memory Away*, by award-winning author Helen R. Myers.

And *next* month, we're beginning CELEBRATION 1000, a very exciting, ultraspecial three-month promotion celebrating the publication of the 1000th Silhouette Desire. During April, May and June, look for books by some of your most beloved writers, including Mary Lynn Baxter, Annette Broadrick, Joan Johnston, Cait London, Ann Major and Diana Palmer, who is actually writing book #1000! These will be months to remember, filled with "keepers."

As always, I wish you the very best,

Lucia Macro
Senior Editor

Please address questions and book requests to:
Silhouette Reader Service
U.S.: 3010 Walden Ave., P.O. Box 1325, Buffalo, NY 14269
Canadian: P.O. Box 609, Fort Erie, Ont. L2A 5X3

HELEN R. MYERS
JUST A MEMORY AWAY

SILHOUETTE *Desire*®
Published by Silhouette Books
America's Publisher of Contemporary Romance

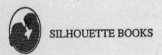 SILHOUETTE BOOKS

ISBN 0-373-05990-6

JUST A MEMORY AWAY

Books by Helen R. Myers

HELEN R. MYERS

satisfies her preference for a reclusive life-style by living deep in the Piney Woods of East Texas with her husband, Robert, and—because they were there first—the various species of four-legged and winged creatures that wander throughout their ranch. To write has been her lifelong dream, and to bring a slightly different flavor to each book is an ongoing ambition.

Admittedly restless, she thinks that helps her writing, explaining, "It makes me reach for new territory and experiment with old boundaries." In 1993 the Romance Writers of America awarded *Navarrone* the prestigious RITA award for Best Short Contemporary Novel of the Year.

For Pam Williams

a special friend "Down Under"

with love and thanks to you and the family
for the friendship and the laughter

Prologue

He'd been driving for hours since he'd stopped in Oklahoma City for lunch, and the miles were beginning to take their toll on him, along with the strain of driving in the dark. Unable to conclude whether his eyes or his butt ached more, he scowled at the green-and-white road sign that became visible on his right. According to it, he still had another ninety-minutes-plus of torture ahead of him before he reached Houston.

Hell. The fuel gauge indicated the car was getting seriously low on gas again, and he couldn't wait much longer before stretching his legs. But except for the out-of-the-way filling station he'd noticed advertised behind that mileage sign, the next major rest stop was a good twenty miles down the road. He doubted the car had that much gas left in it. It served him right for not exiting ten miles back; but no, he'd snubbed that station once he'd recognized its corporate logo. No way had he been willing to give them another dime of his money; not after he'd lost that tidy bundle in the stock market because of them.

Why the devil hadn't he simply flown down to Texas, as he usually did?

Because Sidney said you needed time off.

The first thing he planned to do upon checking in at his hotel was to call his golf-partner-cum-physician and tell him what he could do with himself the next time he got another of his brainstorms. "'Your blood pressure is going through the ceiling,'" he mimicked Sid with disgust. "'Slow down now or the only golf you'll be playing is with the likes of J. Paul Getty and Diamond Jim Brady at that great country club in the sky.'"

So what had he done? When the business trip to Oklahoma City and Houston came up, he'd let Sid talk him into renting a car and driving down from Chicago. *Driving.* "Take time to notice the scenery for a change. Then catch a connecting flight to the Cayman Islands for a week and ingest some sea air. Ease up on the old ticker. Do it for me, okay?"

Well, he had news for Sid; if the Great Accountant in the Sky had wanted him to waste his time taxiing himself along some of the flattest geography in this country, He would never have allowed the invention of supersonic jets.

He sighed with exasperation as he exited for Peavy's Country Store and Gas, thinking that the place damn well better provide the twenty-four-hour service it advertised.

Pine trees towered on either side of him as he coasted to a stop at the unlit crossroads. In fact, he couldn't see a light of any kind in either direction, let alone a hint of any type of man-made structure.

It's enough to make you miss downtown Chicago. At rush hour.

With a long-suffering sigh, he cut a sharp left turn as the advertisement had directed and thought he would like a few words with the environmentalists who kept crying wolf about the world's population dilemma. The only thing in excess around here seemed to be trees.

He drove for about a quarter of a mile. The view didn't change: varying degrees of blackness continued to cocoon him, thanks to the encroaching woods, and all that his headlights picked up was—

"What the...?"

His car's beams illuminated a white compact with its hood raised. But what sent his mood plummeting straight into gloom was seeing that the driver was female.

Just what he needed. More woman problems.

If it had been a guy, he would have kept driving and notified the attendant at the station; but no such luck. The woman stood beside the car waving a white handkerchief or something. Apparently no one had ever told her that it was unsafe to get out of her car at night and flag down strangers.

"Brainless twit. You're a walking crime statistic waiting to happen." Lucky for her, *he'd* come along, because there was only one thing on his mind and it wasn't trouble.

He turned on his emergency flashers and pulled up beside the miniskirted brunette. As he lowered the passenger window at the push of a button, she pressed a hand to her low-necked blouse and leaned over to eye him anxiously.

Now she got cautious? he fumed silently. He didn't bother responding to her tentative smile. "Engine trouble?"

She eyed his attire and visibly relaxed.

"Thank God. I thought I was going to have to spend the whole night stranded out here. Do you know how to change a flat tire, sir?"

He stretched to peer at the compact's front and back wheels. "I don't see any flat."

"It's the front right one. I hate to trouble you."

Right. He watched her abandon demureness to brush her hair back from her face, which gave him a blatant view of generous cleavage and creamy skin swelling over the cups of a lacy black bra. *Sure, you hate to trouble me.*

He sighed. "Save the floor show, honey. I'm in a hurry, but I will drive you to the station down the street. Peavy's, I think the sign said. Someone there should be able to help you."

For an instant her expression hardened, but she quickly replaced it with a beguiling smile. "You're obviously not from around here or you'd know that place went out of business ages ago."

Swearing under his breath, he downshifted, and climbed out of the car. What choice did he have? Contrary to what his last secretary had accused as she'd walked out on him, he wasn't a bastard; just disciplined and busy. In any case, if the woman was a local and knew about Peavy's, maybe she could tell him where the next—

Preoccupied, his senses as numb as his body from the hours of monotonous driving, he was slow to hear someone approaching him from behind, slow to react. He began to turn, only to be stopped by a sharp blow to the back of his head.

The night exploded into dozens of headlights that blinded him. A sonic boom roared in his ears. As panic splintered every bone in his frame, he tried to run; but his legs betrayed him and he toppled to the street.

He knew another savage instant of pain as he hit the oily road. Then he knew nothing at all.

One

"*Frankie*—dance with me!"

"Thank you, Moose. But I value my toes too much to expose them to those clodhoppers of yours. Besides, it's time for last call. Want another beer before you go home for the night?"

He did and he ordered another round for the other two regulars seated with him. Frankie nodded, wheeled around to her next table, and repeated the question.

"I got a better idea, Frankie, darlin'," the potbellied man at the farthest end drawled with a tomcat smile. "Why don't you take me home to that li'l ol' trailer of yours? I've got a powerful hankerin' to be tucked in t'night."

"There's no missing that you need tucking in, Howie," she told him, as she exchanged the filled ashtray on the table for a clean one. "But what would your wife say?"

He grinned and his twinkling eyes vanished in the folds of

his pudgy face. "That you didn't have the sense of a chigger."

Frankie waited for his buddies to stop guffawing and slapping at the table. "Well, you know I do respect Pru's judgment. On top of that, you don't like animals. The man who gets tucked in by me has to be crazy about my pets, too."

"Aw, ain't nobody on earth 'cept you could find those critters lovable, Frankie."

With a shrug and a smile, she collected several long-necked beer bottles and added them to the empties on her tray. "They may not all be as pretty as Lassie or hold a conversation like Mr. Ed, but they're better company than the two-legged critters I've gone out with. Stayed around longer, too," she added with a wink. "Now except for Howie, who's going to have coffee or else have his keys taken, what'll it be, boys?"

A few requested a repeat of their last order, and she returned to the bar and called her list to Benny. As the owner of The Two-Step Club reached into the cooler for the beers, Frankie dropped the empty cans and bottles in their proper recycling drums.

When she'd started working here fourteen months ago, the routine was to toss everything into the industrial garbage receptacle out back. She convinced everyone to separate aluminum from glass. Once a week Benny loaded the barrels into her truck, and she took them to the recycling plant in the next town. Once a month the proceeds were split between owner and employees.

"Sure has been slow since those timber-company fellas moved up the road," Benny muttered, adding a bourbon and water to her tray.

Frankie wrinkled her nose, as much for the cigarette-butt-filled ashtrays she dumped as for his observation. Just because her boss didn't have people stacked three-deep at the bar, he acted as if he had one foot in bankruptcy court. For her part, she didn't miss the timber people's tips.

"Be glad they left while there are still some trees around," she told him, thinking about the mess they'd left behind. She had to pass several of their so-called "cleared sites" on her way to and from work, and they more accurately resembled the aftereffects of a forest fire—or worse.

The skinny man's sailor's cap nearly fell off as he threw back his head and groaned to the ceiling. In the background the jukebox switched from a mournful country-and-western ballad to a bawdy rock-and-roll tune. "Could we skip the environmentalist lecture for once?" He had to all but shout to be heard above the pulsating music. "You wouldn't have so much time to stand on a soapbox if you got yourself a life!"

His declaration was nothing new, but it still didn't bother her. "I have a life."

"You live in an aluminum hot-dog wrapper, you collect garbage, and you commune with terrorist reptiles, rude birds, and neurotic flea-breeding strays."

She eyed him mildly. "To each his own. Do I criticize your customers?"

"Never you mind them. They pay my taxes. What you're doing isn't normal. Look at you. You're young, kinda cute in a short sort of way."

"How many times do I have to tell you that five-five isn't short, it's average."

"Sure, sure, and to a penguin you're a giant. Well, you'd be five-six if you didn't have that mop weighing you down."

As he added the mug of draft beer to the rest, Frankie blew her thick, shaggy bangs out of her eyes, and gave him a benign look. "Now don't let your insecurities get the best of you. I heard all about your disorder on one of those talk shows last week."

"*I* have a disorder?"

With tongue in cheek, she swept up her tray. "In a manner of speaking. You're one of those people who find the easiest way to ignore your own shortcomings is to point out someone else's."

"Who gets to ignore 'em? Me? Ha!" The retired chief petty officer's finger shook as he pointed at her. "I have news for you, Miss Mouth. Estelle keeps a list of my shortcomings on the refrigerator! Disorder, nothing. You're looking at a persecuted man."

With a playful "Aw," Frankie left to deliver the drinks. She performed an abbreviated rendition of the Lambada to maneuver between the tables, secretly admitting to herself that she really didn't mind Benny's nagging. In fact she'd now been in Slocum Springs longer than she'd stayed anywhere since inheriting the Silver Duck from her grandfather five years ago. If Benny had been anything less than a sweetheart, she would have been long gone by now.

Nevertheless, his comments did linger in her mind, and it was what she was thinking about as she left the club an hour later. While driving home she concluded that regardless of how patiently she'd tried, she hadn't yet succeeded in making people appreciate, or at least respect, her philosophy of life.

"Tough cookies," she announced, tired of the subject.

She was twenty-seven years old, for pity's sake. If her ideas didn't come close to what the rest of the world practiced—

"Aaah!"

She hit the brakes, and hoped Petunia had enough left in her to respond. In the last second, she closed her eyes, convinced she was about to flatten the naked man standing in the middle of the road with her ancient truck.

Either the purple pickup's brakes were in better shape than she'd believed, or she owed her guardian angel another debt of gratitude. In any case, Petunia squealed to a halt—inches away from the streaker.

Frankie stared at him. He blinked back at her.

"Well, now...what do we have here?"

This couldn't be an April Fools' prank, because it was months late. It couldn't be a Halloween prank because it was months too early. The guy wasn't wearing some sort of a costume, either; he was honestly naked—save for the handful of cottonwood and oak leaves he held unsteadily in front of his privates.

"Glory be." This wasn't some joke one of her mischievous customers had decided to pull on her. A person would deserve an Academy Award to fake that look of shock and fear.

Oh, yes, he was real, and that kept her from bursting into relieved, giddy laughter. Still, he did look funny in a bizarre, incredible sort of way. And how ironic that on the very evening Benny had lectured her again about her love life, she should get this dubious...offering.

As he hesitantly rounded to her side of the car, she rolled down her window. "Um...Adam, I presume?"

"You know me?"

Oh, brother. Maybe you jumped to one too many conclusions, Jonesy.

"That was a joke," she told him. When he made no response, she decided he might simply be slow. "The leaves and all?" She gestured to his minute ensemble.

His blue eyes remained blank. "Can you help me?"

"I really don't think—"

It was as he began looking around that she had a clear view of the other side of his face and spotted the blood streaking down his right temple. With a gasp, Frankie downshifted and secured her emergency brake. Careful not to knock him off-balance, she nudged him out of the way with her door, and eased out of the truck. Now that she was closer, she could see that he was shaking like a paint mixing machine, which left him none too steady on his feet.

"Holy hiccups, what happened?" she cried, grasping his upper arms to steady him.

"I—I'm not sure. I woke up, and . . . I don't know."

"Where do you come from?"

He looked around again and pointed over Petunia's hood. Since there wasn't a streetlight in sight, all that she could see out there was the ravine dropping off from the shoulder, and the black-on-black shadow indicating the woods beyond.

"Uh-huh." The smell of being set up returned stronger than before. "Who are you?"

He tried to answer. She could tell by the way his facial muscles tightened and he broke out in a sweat. But in the end he simply gave her a confused look.

"Adam?"

She should have suffered whiplash from the way her skepticism switched to concern. Without thinking, she reached up to touch his bruised face. "You poor man. You don't have a clue, do you?"

"No. Do you?"

She shook her head. "But don't worry," she added quickly. "We'll find out in no time at all. First let's get you settled in my truck, and after that I'll go check out the ditch. Surely something's there that will tell us what we want to know."

If he agreed, he kept that to himself, and merely stood there looking as if whatever would come from her mouth

had to be the gospel. Frankie decided it was one thing for
Lambchop to take on that expression when she had to leave
for work; it was another to have a grown man doing it.

With more questions than answers as to what she was
dealing with, she helped him around to the passenger side of
the truck. It wasn't easy. He had to be at least six feet,
maybe a bit more, and he had a sturdy build. No doubt his
mother—or wife, she amended, embarrassed at how neatly
she'd almost avoided that thought—had made sure he didn't
skip too many meals. At the same time, he was well toned.
Taut. She tried not to let her gaze wander to places the leaves
only began to cover, but who could help noticing?

Once she opened the door, she reached inside for the
blanket kept behind the seat. "Here you go. This might itch
a bit. It's Maury's and he tends to shed, but it's all I have."

The stranger looked over her shoulder as if waiting for
someone to protest his having the covering. "I can share."

What *was* she dealing with, here? Once again Frankie
eyed him with suspicion. When she still saw no reason to
think this was a cunning act, she wrapped the blanket
around him and helped him into her vehicle.

She ripped out a few tissues from the mangled box
crunched between the windshield and dashboard, to dab at
the worst of the blood already beginning to dry on the side
of his face. Once she got most of it, she pressed the tissues
into his hand, grabbed her flashlight out of the glove com-
partment, and ran to look for his clothes and whatever else
she might find that would indicate his identity.

She found an empty beer can, an ice-cream stick, and a
number of cigarette butts, which made her grateful they'd
been crushed out when discarded. She didn't, however, find
anything that would help her solve her mystery.

After prolonging her search a bit more, she returned to
the idling truck and paused beside the open passenger door

to consider the shivering stranger. The way he stared back at her made it clear that no matter what she asked him, she wasn't going to be reassured by the answer.

But what a nice face—despite the ugly abrasion on his forehead, a less severe one on his cheek, and the dirt and weeds in his brown hair. He had a face that spoke of strength and frankness, centered by an Anglo-straight nose, balanced by a wide, generous mouth, and punctuated with a slightly stubborn chin.

It was his mouth that drew her attention most. With the slightest smile, he would undoubtedly steal hearts. With the grimmest frown, he would undoubtedly scare the hush puppies out of anyone. If she'd been the betting type, she would have bet tonight's tips that this was the man everyone in school would have voted Most Likely to Succeed. Here was the guy no girl ever forgot, even if she never got lucky enough to date him. No doubt some woman somewhere was beginning to pace the floors and chew her fingernails to nubs with worry over him.

Frankie felt another pinch in the area of her heart, and in self-defense shifted her attention to the large-boned hands that clutched at the blanket. He wore no ring, which meant nothing; these days guys were professionals at hiding such minor technicalities as wives and children. But surely this man wasn't one of those? Why else would she have such a powerful impulse to say, "Finders keepers"? He was definitely keeper material.

"I'd better get you to the hospital," she told him, concerned that she'd let her fantasy go too—

"No!"

His sharp response stopped her from shutting the door. "Look, you're hurt. You need medical attention."

"You. You help me."

As charming as this you-Jane-me-Tarzan dialogue was, it was starting to wear thin. "Listen, gorgeous, it doesn't take a medical degree to see that this is more than a kiss-and-make-it-better situation."

"You."

He had no idea what he was asking of her. Shaking her head, she took the tissues from him—he hadn't done a thing with them, anyway—and once again dabbed gently around his worst wound. "I don't know why you're making this difficult for me."

"Just need to rest." He winced, and shifted slightly away from her.

"That's what I'm trying to tell you. At a hospital you could. And they would contact the police, who would—"

"*Please.*"

Frankie stopped dabbing and leaned close to look deeper into his eyes for a clue as to what was going on. In the dim overhead light the color wasn't exactly dark like a deep-water blue, but more of a slate or stormy shade. Of course, some of that gray could be a result of the concussion or whatever it was that he was suffering from. In any case, it bothered her to be tempted to find out how they would look in the light of day, or when he was healthy. Smiling.

Stop it, Jonesy. You don't need the trouble or the heart-ache.

Nevertheless, she heard herself murmur, "I guess I could take you down the road to my place. But I should warn you, it's not fancy."

"I only want to lie down. Get warm."

He was cold? She'd thought he'd been shaking from the fright she'd given him, and from whatever he'd gone through that had put him in this state. After all, it was July, and it had to be at least seventy degrees or better. That more than anything else decided her.

She tossed the soiled tissues onto the floorboard, and carefully shut the passenger door. When she once again slid behind the steering wheel, she shot him a wry look.

"Maybe I'd better warn you about a few more things. I don't live alone."

He seemed confused for a moment, but soon inclined his head. "I won't stay. Just . . . rest."

Maybe it was wishful thinking, but she could have sworn he looked disappointed. "You misunderstand. I mean that you won't quite have the privacy you might want, because I have pets and they, um, get around."

"I like dogs and cats. I think."

She chuckled softly and shifted into gear. "Well, that's a start."

They drove a few miles, and during that time Frankie waited, hoping he would initiate more conversation, but he didn't. He simply sat beside her. The shaking eased a bit; nevertheless, it didn't stop entirely.

"I'd turn on the heater for you, but it doesn't work. Neither does the air conditioner. Petunia has a few miles on her." She patted the truck's worn dashboard with affection.

Her companion merely peered into the dark night, as if trying to recognize something of his surroundings.

In an attempt to help him relax—and maybe herself, too—she offered, "My name is Frankie."

That got his attention. "Why do you have a boy's name?"

"Blame it on my mother." Frankie made a face. "When she was a kid, she dreamed of being an actress. Not only didn't that happen, she ended up marrying my father and inherited the last name of Jones. What a curse for poor Mom. All during her pregnancy with me, she went through book after book of baby names, until she came up with Francesca.''

"Francesca . . . pretty."

Ugh. He would say something like that. "It's not bad," she said with hard-won grace, "but not for someone like me. Before I was five, I had everyone calling me Frankie."

Her passenger went back to studying his surroundings. Almost as an afterthought he murmured, "I don't know if I like my name."

Boy, she'd all but stuck her whole leg in it that time. Frankie shot him an apologetic look. "Don't worry. No doubt all you need is a good night's rest." Belatedly, however, she remembered having read somewhere that you weren't supposed to let a concussion victim drift into too deep a sleep. She decided she would let the experts warn him about that when she finally got him to the hospital.

It took only another few minutes to reach her home. The Silver Duck was parked on the southwest boundary of Mr. Miller's farm. Mr. Miller was a widower who owned several hundred acres bordering a creek that fed into the Trinity River. That creek also filled the stock pond where Frankie had parked her trailer. Her agreement with the old-timer was that she watched over his southernmost boundary—he'd often been the victim of poachers and cattle rustlers—and in exchange, he let her tie into the utility box that he'd set up for a former ranch hand, who hadn't stayed on.

No sooner did she park beside the hail-damaged and time-worn trailer than they found themselves surrounded by a small herd of animals. Amid the barking, meowing and general ruckus, Frankie noted her passenger's wide-eyed stare at the three-legged cat that stared back at him through the windshield.

She grinned. "Don't worry. This only looks and sounds like Little Big Horn. I assure you, they're all fairly friendly.

Hello, babies,'' she cooed, as she eased open her door. The animals swarmed around her to nuzzle, lick, and playfully nip at her jeans and T-shirt.

When Frankie made it to the passenger side and opened the door to help out her newest houseguest, he hesitated. ''I thought you said dogs and cats?''

''No, you did.''

And there *was* a dog and cat. Maury, named after a TV talk-show host, was a long-haired German shepherd, blinded in one eye from a carelessly aimed BB gun. The cat was Callie, short for Calico, who often acted as mother to the group, despite her handicap, the result of a near-fatal car accident.

There was also Samson, the potbellied pig, who used his girth to push his way into anywhere he wanted to go. George, a rather distinguished muskovy duck. Her beloved Lambchop, the clubfooted donkey, who brought up the rear of every family parade. And perhaps her most irascible member of the family, Rasputin, a goat with eyebrows as bushy as his long beard.

Once the stranger emerged from the truck, Maury and Rasputin initiated an instant tug-of-war with the blanket. Frankie sighed; she should have known they wouldn't cut the new guy any slack.

''Guys, guys...not *now!*''

She gave her crew gentle nudges with her knees and elbows, whatever worked as she assisted her guest up the two steps to the deck she'd built herself last fall. For the most part, though, her efforts to keep her brood away from her guest were wasted. By the time she had the trailer door open, she had a feeling her company was wondering if he wouldn't have been better off risking a night out under the stars beating off mosquitoes and God knew what else. She didn't know how to warn him that he was in for round two, except to simply push open the door.

"I'm home!" she called into the darkness.

Even before she found the light switch, she was greeted with a scream. "*Erk*...save me! Save me!"

From across the room she heard a flutter of wings, and then felt claws grip her shoulder with flawless precision. "Ouch—watch it!" Frankie muttered, flicking on the wall switch.

As the room flooded with light, illuminating the crimson-and-azure parrot on her shoulder, the bird gave her a peck on the cheek. "*Erk*. Hello, Blondie."

"You know you're not supposed to let yourself out until I tell you it's safe."

"*Erk*. Gimmee a kiss."

Although she complied, Frankie didn't spare the bird a necessary scolding. "What I should do is let Dr. J. have you for dinner, you juvenile delinquent."

That was too many words for the creature, and yet Honey seemed to get the message. She glided back across the room and into her cage, quickly tugging the door shut behind her. Just in time, too. Right on her tail came Dr. J., the Manx cat who'd recently come close to successfully slam-dunking the parrot into his food bowl.

"I really do work at keeping these two separated," she told her guest, who stood mesmerized by the show. "But Dr. J.'s learned how to escape from the back bedroom, and I haven't figured out what to do about that yet."

"Are there any more?" the stranger asked, glancing around warily.

"Two. But you won't meet them until they're ready. They're very shy." She took his arm again. "Why don't we get you cleaned up? We can talk more after. The bathroom's the first door," she said, pointing down the hall.

"As for clothes...I'm afraid you'll have to cope with the blanket, or a towel. I do have some sleep shirts, but somehow I don't think even they'd be large enough."

The stranger paused, and although he needed the support of the wall to stay on his feet, his gaze was direct—and grateful. "I may be confused, but...I know I'm asking for a great deal from you."

Mercy, she could spend all night and more gazing into those eyes. "That's okay."

"Too much trust."

"That's okay," she repeated, not caring if she did sound like a just-hatched chick.

He didn't quite sigh, but he might as well have. "Thank you."

The longer he watched her, the more active her imagination grew, until she began feeling her insides turn to taffy, her cheeks grow feverish. She gestured into the bathroom, while backing toward the kitchen. "I, um, have to feed the gang. Don't drown in there, okay?"

"Miss...Frankie?"

She stopped. Waited.

"You won't go too far? You...the sound of your voice...you're very reassuring."

Oh, help.

Right then and there she knew she was in major trouble. Between the lost tone in his voice and the look in his eyes, he might as well have put a one-armed nelson around her heart. Frankie could deal with mashers, professional flirts, and even a male-chauvinist porky, but a vulnerable man clearly in trouble...?

"Drat it and phooey. I thought you guys were extinct!"

"Wh— Extinct?"

This was not a time to knock him into a tailspin with her impulsive philosophizing. Frankie dismissed herself with a wave. "Never mind. Everybody feels as if they're lost once in a while. Go take that shower, and we'll take things from there. Okay?"

Two

The instant she heard him shut the bathroom door, Frankie pursed her lips together for a silent whistle. What a close call! If he'd stood there another few seconds, no doubt she would have offered to bathe him herself. Boy, if the guy could do that to her when dazed and grubby, there was no telling what impact he would have when spruced up and functioning on all eight cylinders.

Bemused by the prospect, she headed back toward the kitchen, only to stop at the sudden touch of hot breath on her cheek. It was followed by the flick of a sandpaper tongue, then the weight of two reptilian feet. Finally, the iguana climbed off a stereo speaker to wrap himself completely around her shoulders.

Frankie scratched Bugsy under his flabby neck. "So what do you think?" she whispered, continuing on her way. "I know you're intrigued. You never come out to check out company unless you are."

At the counter she stooped to let the iguana onto the steadier base, then flipped on more lights. Dr. J. was already settled on his favorite bar stool in the hope of getting a late-night snack, and Honey croaked from her cage, although she still had plenty in her feeder to nibble on.

"Okay, you guys," Frankie said, conscious of the less patient scratching and braying that hadn't stopped just beyond the screen door. "Everyone will get something, as usual, but keep it down. Mercy... far be it from you guys to wait five extra minutes while I try to take care of a guest!"

Maury uttered a low-throated growl through the screen. He always needed to get in the last word.

"I heard that." Frankie held up the steak bone she'd brought from work that one of the girls had saved for her. "See this? No jealousy or I'll let Samson chew on this."

That earned her a snort of disgust from Maury, who then slapped the aluminum door with a huge paw. Rasputin supplied his support with a bump of his head.

Frankie couldn't help but smile. No wonder her guest had looked dubious about getting out of Petunia. Even for someone familiar with them and as fond as she was, they could be a challenge. She knew she wouldn't be able to play with them tonight as much as she would like, either, because she needed to save a bit of energy for the man who remained too quiet in the bathroom.

Despite her intentions, it took her a good twenty minutes to feed the motley group. By the time she issued "lovies" to the last animal, and returned to the bathroom, the prospect of a shower looked pretty good to her, too. Hoping that the stranger had finished, she knocked lightly on the door.

"How's it going in there?"

She listened, but heard no reply.

"Hello? Are you all right?"

The silence had her imagining the worst: what if he'd been injured more severely than she'd imagined? What if he'd lost his balance and was bleeding to death on her bathroom floor? What if...?

"Mister! I'm going to come in, okay?"

When he still failed to answer, Frankie momentarily lost her confidence. Only darn it all, she couldn't afford to; there was no one to do this if she didn't!

As she cautiously peered around the door, she found her guest seated on the commode lid. He looked much the same as when she'd left him.

Not one to stifle too many emotions, she sighed and touched his shoulder gently so as not to startle him. "Hey. Didn't you hear me?"

He looked up at her, and her heart did a little jig as his eyes brightened, warmed. "Hello," he murmured.

"Hi. You're supposed to be taking a shower."

He glanced at the stall as if only now realizing its purpose. "I guess I forgot."

Forgot the only instruction she'd given him? Frankie's spirits sank again. "Please, don't say that. You don't know how close I am to calling the police for help."

"No. No...don't."

"But you're hurt, and it's obvious this didn't happen by simply falling over a tree stump. I could probably be put in jail for the infraction of some civil law by not already having you at a hospital. Failure to render aid or something—I seem to remember they have that law here."

He frowned. "But you did help me."

"Proper. Proper aid is the key word in this case." Frankie crouched before him to make him meet her studious gaze. "Look...you have to work with me. You have to take that shower. You'll feel much better if you get cleaned up, I'm sure of it. If not, I'll let you lie down for a while afterward. You really don't want to lie down on my clean sheets when you're caked with mud and who knows what else, right? Can you do that for me?"

He inclined his head. It wasn't, however, a full-fledged nod.

Not sure that he fully comprehended, Frankie gestured toward the fiberglass cubicle. "Well...anytime you're ready."

Obviously it wasn't now. Her guest simply continued sitting there staring straight ahead.

Beginning to feel as if she was fighting an unwinnable battle, she took hold of his hands, which hung loosely between his knees. "Let me try a different approach.... Are you making sense of anything I'm saying?"

"Yes."

"Then what's the problem?"

"I don't want to go in there."

Frankie eyed the shower stall. What did he mean? Sure, her trailer didn't look like much from the outside, even through the kind filter of darkness. After the death of her grandmother, her grandfather had towed the thing from one part of the States to another and then some, not missing a single pothole or dusty canyon on his journey of self-discovery. And there was no use trying to ignore the obvious: she could almost open her own zoo. That had its own cost. But concussion or no concussion, surely he could tell she was a painstaking housekeeper?

"I don't understand," she told him with quiet urgency.

"It looks— I can't see."

"See what?"

"*See*. In there."

It took her a few seconds, but she finally understood what he meant. He would feel claustrophobic in the stall. Whether this was a result of his injury, or something deeper, she had no way of knowing; but it didn't appear as if she was going to be able to talk him out of it before the sun rose.

"Holy Moly..." She sat back on her heels. "I'm definitely in way over my head here. You have to let me take you somewhere."

"No."

"To a doctor? For your own good?"

"No!"

Before she could react, he took possession of her wrists in a blood-draining grasp. He had impressive strength for an injured guy; in fact, his touch was so intense she had to bite back a cry. Sure, she'd been clawed, bitten and bullied time and again by the strays and abused animals she'd taken into her home; but this was different. This was more personal, more dangerous than anything she'd experienced before.

"Listen to me." Ever so slowly, she lowered her head so that her cheek stroked against the powerful fingers shutting off the blood supply to her hands. "You're hurting me...and you're frightening me."

He immediately let her go. Looking shocked, he touched her hair. "I didn't mean to. I'm so sorry."

The anguish in his voice was real, his touch gentle. Frankie abandoned her momentary impulse to run; however, she did sit up and eye him with renewed concern. "What am I going to do with you? Don't you understand that you have to get cleaned up and get that dirt out of your wounds?"

He frowned, looked at the shower stall and then at her again. "Can you help me?"

Whoa.

He couldn't be serious? But no sooner did Frankie open her mouth to tell him that, than she realized she didn't have a choice. This wasn't an act. "Aw...no," she moaned, "don't do this to me."

"Please. It's not what you're thinking. I'm just not sure I can—"

"Manage on your own in such a small space?" At his brief nod, she groaned inwardly. Granted, the male body was hardly an unknown commodity to her, but she hadn't seen all that many. Did he realize what he was asking of her?

Of course he did, she realized a moment later when a dark flush crept into his face. Otherwise he wouldn't look as miserable and trapped as she felt.

She sighed. "Am I a wuss or what?"

"Sorry?"

"*Anyone* can be a marshmallow," she said, rising to slide open the shower door and turn on the water. "It takes a rare talent to be a wuss."

From the cabinet behind her, she took the biggest towel she owned and set it on the edge of the sink for when they were done. Then she slipped out of her sneakers.

"Let's get one thing straight," she told the injured stranger as she tugged off her socks. "Any funny business and you're dead meat, got it?"

"Not feeling very funny."

"We'll see."

She didn't turn away from him as she stripped off her jeans. Modesty wasn't the issue; and despite her comment, she didn't think he looked as if he was in any shape to really pull something. What's more her T-shirt and panties left her more covered than when swimming with Holly at her friend's apartment pool.

It was the stranger who presented the problem.

"Okay," she said, adjusting the hot-and cold-water taps. "I guess I'm ready if you are."

Frankie's curiosity as to whether he was the modest type or not was answered seconds after she spoke. The stranger used her shoulder and the wall for support, and eased himself to his feet. The abandoned blanket simply fell away, and he stood before her as naked and unsteady as a one-year-old testing his legs for the first time.

And you thought keeping something on would make things less sexual? Jonesy, you are daffier than Honey.

She already considered the man a heartthrob, but that proved the father of all understatements. He was what the girls at the club would call a "stud." Simply beautiful, as far as she was concerned. One inevitable cheater-glance downward, and she knew it would be a miracle if she got through this without making an absolute fool of herself.

She slipped an arm around his waist to offer additional balance. "Easy. Easy." She coaxed him into the stall. "You're doing great."

"Feel lousy."

"There's a built-in seat in here. You can sit down in just a second."

"Okay, just ... don't close the door."

"I won't." Things were cramped enough as it was. She'd never thought about how small the shower was in all the time she'd owned the Silver Duck. But the stranger changed that the instant they were both inside the cubicle and she tried to help him onto the triangular bench. It was impossible. No matter how badly she wanted to avoid it, those long legs of his were tantamount to trying to maneuver around redwood trees in a gym locker. If she wanted to get him settled, not to mention cleaned up, she would have to suffer through a bit more body contact.

Tough work, Jonesy, but you are the only volunteer.

"Wait a minute." Already wet, she was drenched by the time she maneuvered him to where he needed to be. "And we haven't even been properly introduced," she muttered, the third and hopefully last time his nose bumped against her breast.

Fortunately, he either didn't hear her or else didn't care to comment, and she quickly busied herself by adjusting the spray away from herself and back onto him. "Now, if you get dizzy or anything, hold on to me."

For the moment, however, he seemed content to lean back against the fiberglass wall and close his eyes. In fact, he looked as if it would take dynamite to move him again.

That troubled her. "You can't go to sleep on me."

"Tired."

"No, no, no. You have to help me to help you."

"Try..."

She shook her wet hair out of her eyes and decided to work on his hair first. From the looks of the dirty water running down his face, she figured the sooner they got him cleaned up there, the better his chances of avoiding an infection in those cuts and scrapes.

Fortunately she used a fragrance-free shampoo and soap, so she didn't have to worry about an allergic reaction; but she did worry about causing him additional pain. She asked him several times as she carefully worked the soap into a rich lather whether she was hurting him or not, until she finally believed he meant it when he said she had an "angel's touch."

"I sure hope so," she said, getting more chatty to keep from focusing on how his thighs kept rubbing against hers. "I'd sure hate trying to explain to the police why I thought I could do a better job at patching you up than a hospital could."

"No police. No hospital."

"Yeah, yeah. I heard you before."

Once she rinsed out the shampoo, however, she had to sacrifice gentleness for thoroughness. Although she half drowned him, she used a washcloth to clean the wound at his temple; but, under the circumstances, it was the only way to make sure she got out every bit of grit.

By the time she had him lean forward to focus on the lump at the back of his head, he'd lost what was left of his equilibrium. When she released him to rinse out her cloth, he almost fell off the seat, nearly taking her with him.

She earned a bruised elbow for that one and a near heart attack. Once she got him steady, she tried again...and again. Each time, she had to deal with the same results.

"I know you're beat," she gasped, wearying herself, "but we have to get done."

"Feel...sick."

"Now, is that any way to talk to the woman who's considering having your baby?" She peered at him, hoping that little shocker might have the desired effect. It didn't. "Okay, then let's try this. Brace your forearms on your knees and your forehead here." She patted her tummy to show him.

At first the solution worked perfectly. He stayed steady, and she made good progress as she attended to the nasty bump on the back of his head.

Then she grew aware of how much hotter his breath was than the water—against her tummy...her thighs.... And as if that wasn't enough, when he tilted off-balance again, he recovered by grabbing her legs!

Frankie froze, the feel of his big, strong hands moving on the backs of her thighs just a teensy bit more than she'd bargained for. "Um...mister."

Could he be toying with her, after all? When he shifted his hold higher and almost cupped her bottom, she was nearly convinced. Then, just as she aimed the washcloth to slap his hands away, he uttered a deep, miserable moan.

"Can't do this much longer."

That makes two of us. But she forgave him. "Hold on. We're almost through."

"Too much trouble."

"No, you're a good sport." *Better than me.*

"*You.* And you have...hands."

She smiled. "There's something else we have in common."

"Great. Meant great hands."

The fragmented compliment was another throwaway. He was grateful, that's all; and yet a sharp little thrill raced through her. She was beginning to enjoy this a bit too much.

She tried to be discreet as she put some distance between them and concentrated on washing his neck and shoulders, his chest and arms. It didn't help. How was she supposed to ignore that although he was on the pale side, his body had the well-developed tone of an athlete?

"Do you run, maybe on an indoor track? Work out at a gym?"

He was slow to answer. "Wish I knew."

There it was again—that hesitant, anxious tone. As she dealt with yet another wave of sympathy for him, she forced a cheery note into her own voice. "I hate exercise myself. It's crazy, because I'm going all the time. But tell me that I have to do some formal physical training and I turn into an amoeba. Almost failed gym in school."

The stranger merely sighed.

It didn't matter. They were finished anyway. Or finished enough. "Why don't we get you to your feet."

She instructed him how to stand, like before, and once again she tried to steady him. He had been a handful earlier; however, it took all her strength this time. As a result, there was no avoiding absolute intimacy—her breasts being crushed against his muscular torso, her cheek against the heavy thud of his heart, and lower...

Omigosh!

No longer was the stranger in a daze. At least one part of him was wide awake! He sucked in a sharp breath, as if only now realizing the problem himself.

"Here." Once she had him out of the stall, she leaned him against the damp tile wall and reached for the towel. She needed to think, and she would do that better if they put something between them.

He seemed as eager to get the thick length of material around his waist as she was. But he also tried to catch her eye. "Frankie—"

"Careful where you step. We've made quite a puddle leaving the door open like we did."

"Frankie."

Blast him, but the man was persistent. "What?"

"Why won't you let me...? I apologize."

Yes, she was a wuss. She had only to hear his anguish, see the concern in his poor battered face, and she instantly turned into mush inside. And all this time she'd thought only animals could do that to her.

"Apologize for what? Being human?" She looked up at him and accepted another truth about his condition. "You're not going to be able to endure another move tonight, are you?"

"Just want to... rest."

"I know. Stay put."

She'd been right about the hunch of letting him lie down on her bed. She knew what to do now.

In the bedroom she flipped on only the small reading lamp, out of concern for his eyes. Then she folded back the coverlet from her queen-size bed and tugged down the sheet. Without trying, her imagination pictured him there, naked between her fresh sheets.

Get over it, Jonesy.

"I know you're not quite dry," she said upon her return to the bathroom. "But you won't hurt anything. The important thing is to get you off your feet. You look ready to drop."

She helped him to her room and into her bed, where as soon as she made him comfortable, she realized his forehead was bleeding again. Rushing back to the bathroom, she got her first-aid kit. Luckily she kept it well stocked for her animals.

Once she had him patched up, all the while chatting away like a computer phone recording, she thought of something else to do. "Aspirin. Your head has to be throbbing by now."

She was gone and back in a flash. After feeding him the pill, she set the cup of water on the table beside the bed in case he got thirsty later.

"Can you think of anything else you might need?"

"No. Yes. Frankie, I didn't want—"

Here they went again. "Try to get some rest now," she said, not wanting to let him finish. She knew what he was going to say, and it was better left alone. She began to rise. "Don't hesitate to call if you start feeling worse. I usually stay up for a while after I get home. I don't need much sleep."

"Francesca, *stop.*"

Who had a choice? Despite his condition, he'd moved faster than Samson when the little oinklet spotted anything edible, and now he had firm hold of her wrist. Wary but resigned, Frankie sat down on the edge of the bed. "What?"

"God, you make me dizzy."

If only he knew his effect on her.

"You have to let me speak," he continued.

"You don't need to be speaking, you need to be resting."

"But you're still not— Don't be afraid of me."

He was too sharp for his own good. "May I remind you that you're the one with the busted head and the Vacant sign flashing on and off in your eyes?"

"Frankie..." He looked as if he wanted to argue with her, but the effort was clearly more than he had to give. "You're a very sweet and...sexy lady."

This was what she'd really been afraid of; that he would say something considerate and tender when she was already reacting way too strongly to him. What's more, the man not only had amnesia, he was blind as a bat! She'd caught a glimpse of herself in the vanity mirror. She looked about as appealing as Callie the time Maury had inadvertently pushed the cat off the dock and into the pond. She'd had no time to brush out her hair, and what little makeup she'd been wearing had either washed off or smeared.

"I'd better go," she said, attempting to gently pry his fingers from around her wrist. She might as well have tried to reshape tungsten steel with a feather.

"I may not know who I am, but I don't think— I *know* I would never hurt you."

Frankie went still, and reluctantly met his troubled gaze. She knew that he told her the truth. At least, as he understood it. But he couldn't know how that only served to add to her sense of wonder about him, about what was happening between them.

"I believe you," she said, able to do nothing but accept the soft and achy feelings churning inside her. "Now will you please try to get some rest?"

He did ease his grip, but he didn't release her completely.

A helpless laugh bubbled up her throat. "What's wrong now?"

"You're really going to leave me?"

"I'll be in the next room."

"Not yet."

"You *have* to sleep."

"I know. But... you make it bearable."

"'It'?"

"Not knowing who... what I am."

That had to be terrifying. She couldn't imagine such a predicament herself, and she only had to look at him to see how it was tearing him up inside. That made chopped meat of the rest of her determination to put some distance between them.

"Keep telling yourself that this is only temporary," she said, keeping her voice low and soothing. "Tomorrow you'll probably open your eyes and, except for one humdinger of a headache, be as good as new. They do say the mind can do the most amazing things when it comes to healing and survival."

"What if I'm not that lucky?"

"Wrong attitude. My gramps used to say, 'Never let the negative gremlins get hold of you. Think of the possibilities and that's half the battle.'" Frankie grinned at his dubious look. "It's true. He had the best outlook on life, and I rarely saw him depressed or angry."

"That explains you."

"Oh, I'm a grouch in comparison."

"Doubt it." The stranger let his eyes drift shut. "You... lived with him?"

"Sometimes. As much as I could. My parents didn't always approve. They didn't understand the wanderlust that drove him, especially after my grandmother died. I had to settle for brief summer visits as a kid, until I got out of school and moved in with him. We had a wonderful time for a while. He passed away five years ago."

"Parents?"

"They're still back east in Pittsburgh, in the brownstone they bought shortly after they were married. My father is with a big insurance company. My mother is... Well, she buys things at garage and estate sales, polishes them up and sells them at a profit to her friends."

"Your grandfather... whose?"

"Whose...oh! Whose parent? Mother's. And she's never stopped apologizing to my father and brothers."

"How many brothers?"

Goodness, he was tenacious. What besides two knocks on the head did it take to put him out of action? "Four. Carson, Blake, Jason and Pierce. I'm the runt of the litter. An accident, actually. Mr. and Mrs. Jones had a little too much sparkling wine on their twelfth wedding anniversary, and nine months later, there I was. The bane of everyone's existence."

"Exaggeration."

"Oh, it's true. I played better bridge than Mom, better poker than Dad. You could never catch me to spank me, and I deserved more than a few. I got better grades in school, even while maintaining the largest paper route in our county, and just when my father had himself convinced that I was going to get through college and become something traditional like a teacher or nurse, I dropped out and began traveling with Gramps. My father wouldn't speak to me for weeks."

The story went over well. The stranger almost smiled. His breathing also was growing slower, deeper. Frankie began to inch off the bed.

He opened his eyes. "What do you do?"

"I'm an unapologetic underachiever now. I work at The Two-Step." At his frown, she explained that it was a bar and grill on the other side of the interstate. "Far enough so that we don't get any of its traffic, which makes it difficult for Benny, my boss, to keep a cook, so the 'grill' part isn't always accurate."

"Wonder what I do."

Frankie didn't like the tense note that had reentered his voice and endeavored to keep things light. "Well, you sure don't mess with dirt-loving critters the way I do." To prove it, she placed her hand next to his. Besides the obvious differences in size, hers displayed the short, sometimes-chipped nails and scratches that came from loving her pets too much.

The stranger stared at his hand. "He even took my ring."

"What ring?" Frankie gasped.

"I don't know. It just feels so...naked."

A ring. The possibility that he had a wife, children waiting somewhere grew stronger. What were they going through tonight?

She would have liked pursuing the subject, but she could see it was having a debilitating effect on her patient. "That does it. Enough talking," she told him, and rose. "Now you try to sleep."

"You'll stay close?"

At the rate he was tying knots in her emotions, he would be lucky if she let him go tomorrow. She always had time in her day and room in her heart to take in another lost or injured soul.

"Right on the couch, but sometimes not even that far, because I am going to have to wake you every once in a while to make sure you don't slip into a coma."

"Thanks."

"One thing—if you need to get up at any time, call me. I don't want you to, um, accidentally step on something. In this place it's likely to bite in return."

He looked a bit disturbed about that. "I'll call."

"Good night. Sleep well."

"Frankie?"

She'd gotten as far as the door. Real progress. "Yes?"

"Nothing. I just wanted to say your name. To make sure there was one thing I remembered when I wake again."

She couldn't answer because of the lump that lodged in her throat. But she thought of that unknown family again, and she knew an intense pang of envy. She hoped that whoever they were, if they existed, they knew how very lucky they were.

Three

___

Frankie kept her word, and over the next few hours checked on him frequently—partly out of concern that one of the animals might sneak into the back room and add to the few gray hairs he already had. But she also stayed close because of the man himself; aware that she was dealing with something unique here, something more complicated than anything she'd ever dealt with before.

If she was smart, she would have used the time he slept to dash over to Mr. Miller's and ask him to call the sheriff's office for her. The old man had become like a surrogate grandfather to her, allowing her to have her mail delivered to his place, and even taking calls from her family, because she refused to be bothered with a telephone. He wouldn't have minded the ungodly hour, not once he recognized Petunia's coughy-cranky engine.

She could have put an end to this, before it got out of

hand. Before she let the dreamer in her get too much control of her imagination. But she didn't.

Every half hour or so, she returned to the bedroom to gently rouse him, give him a drink of water, get him to say a few words. Afterward, she would brush his ash brown hair from his bandaged forehead, and softly encourage him to close his eyes and go back to sleep. He responded so well. Like a child. How could she leave him?

He finalized her decision the last time she checked on him. No sooner did she set the cup back on the nightstand, than he took hold of her hand and wouldn't let go.

"I opened my eyes before," he mumbled, his voice thick with sleep. "You weren't here."

"You only had to call me, and I would have come right away."

That wasn't good enough for him. He refused to release her.

She told him about how it was now past her bedtime. Fatigue was beginning to set in and she yearned for the length of the couch, old and lumpy though it was, not to mention hot due to its foam cushions and her lack of air-conditioning. "If I don't lie down for a bit, I'm going to fall flat on my face come morning when you and everyone else around here will be wanting breakfast," she told him, stifling a yawn.

To her surprise, he patted the vacant side of the bed. "I'll share," he told her for the second time tonight.

If he had been anyone else, she would have laughed in his face. As much as she loved people and tried to give everyone the benefit of the doubt, that didn't mean she had the naiveté of a just-hatched chick. Yet instinctively she knew that despite their earlier reaction to each other, there was only one thing the stranger wanted from her right now.

Without another moment's hesitation, she circled to the far side of the bed. "Keep it up and I'll nominate you for sainthood," she said, gratefully stretching out beside him.

"Want some of the sheet?"

Although she'd changed into a dry sleeper T-shirt, which was anything but suggestive, the thought of being under the same sheet with his stunning, naked body threatened to wipe the thought of sleep completely out of her mind. "That's all right," she murmured, curling into a fetal position with her back to him. "I'm fine. Sweet dreams."

She must have fallen asleep quickly, because the next thing she knew the room was bathed in sunlight and a hand—a large, male hand—had a manacle grip on her thigh. Her heart thudded in sudden panic as she remembered. Everything.

What was he *doing?* Had she been wrong after all?

Not sure what to expect, she rolled over, startled to find her bedmate looking as if he was facing a firing squad himself. For good reason, she realized, once she followed his gaze.

While he attempted to push the bed's headboard through the trailer's wall, a boa constrictor inched up between his legs. It looked particularly ominous when it flicked out its forked tongue.

With a sigh, Frankie rose onto one elbow, snatched the snake, and brought it up to her face. "Stretch, you terrorist. I told you no funny stuff until you were properly introduced." She scooped him up in both hands and carried him down the hall to his bed beneath the couch. "Bad snake. You're lucky our company's last name isn't Robespierre. Now stay there until I apologize on your behalf."

Since she was already close, she detoured to the kitchen to switch on the coffeemaker. On the way back to the bedroom, she let Dr. J. outside, patted Bugsy and uncovered Honey's cage.

"I'm sorry," she said to the man who remained frozen where she'd left him. "That was Stretch. He's usually much friendlier. Most of the time you can use him as a pillow and he won't care." She did, however, keep her fingers crossed behind her back as she made that claim, for as well as she and Stretch got along, he liked to toy with Honey's cage and Dr. J.'s mind, whenever the opportunity presented itself.

"You live with a snake?"

"A baby one. Barely more than three feet." When her guest's expression remained glazed, she added, "It's not as though he's a cobra or a rattler."

"You mean he'll get *bigger?*"

"He's a boa," she said, as if that explained everything. It certainly did to her. "But I won't have him much longer. I took him in when a friend at the club found him in her bathroom after work one night. She lives in a pretty wild apartment complex, so there's no telling how he got in there. At any rate, as much as I love him, I do have a problem with his dietary needs."

"What does he eat? No, never mind," her guest replied with a feeble gesture. "I don't want to know."

"Mmm. Not wise before breakfast. The zoo in Houston said they'd be happy to take him. I just have to wait for them to tell me that they have his new home ready. It will be good knowing he'll have friends, because he does enjoy company."

The stranger closed his eyes.

Frankie used the opportunity to study him. He looked both better and worse this morning; his coloring was better, but his injuries appeared angrier in the light of day. Unable to harness all of her caretaker instincts, she crossed over to him, settled on the edge of the bed and touched his forehead. Her fingers were twice as tanned as his pale, broad forehead.

"Your fever's gone," she murmured, sensitive to how strong his pull was when she got this close. "How do you feel?"

"As if there should be an ax sticking out of my head. Is there?"

"No, no ax, but..." Frankie noticed that the bandage at the back of his head had come off in his sleep, and she retrieved it while gently checking the injury with her other hand. "Oh, poor man. That's one humongous Easter egg you have back there. No wonder your hurting. I'll get you more aspirin as soon as we put something in your stomach. The good news is that there doesn't seem to be any more bleeding."

"Did I mess up your bed?" He began to twist around, only to wince at the sudden move.

"Easy." Frankie stopped him with a fleeting touch to his cheek. "Don't worry about blood. I'm an expert at stains and stuff. I have to be, or else I'd be replacing my clothes every week. Is the pain receding? Maybe you better lie back down."

"It doesn't hurt so much when you're with me."

How could anyone who looked like next month's centerfold for a women's pinup magazine be this sweet? She hesitated, but knew she had to ask. "Do you remember my name?"

Slate-blue eyes that should probably have seemed cold and hard warmed as he took in her sleep-tousled hair, her rumpled T-shirt and tanned, bare legs. "Frankie."

She could have kissed him. "And your name?"

He tried. She could see it in the way the veins swelled at

his temples, the way the muscles around his mouth and along his neck tensed. But in the end he could only make a negative movement with his head.

"Nothing?"

"Adam...?" he murmured, looking confused. "I remember hearing or dreaming the name Adam."

Frankie grimaced. "That was a joke. I called you that last night when I found you, because you were— Never mind."

She might as well have been talking to herself. As soon as he saw he'd guessed wrong about his name, he sank back against the pillows and draped an arm across his eyes. "God. I feel as if I'm losing my mind. Maybe I have lost it along with my memory."

"Stop that! You are as sane as any man I've ever met," she retorted, firmly. "Maybe saner. You've just had a terrible injury."

He lowered his arm. "What am I going to do?"

How did he expect her to think when he looked at her as if she were his entire universe? Under the circumstances, Frankie could think of only one kind of response, pragmatic though it was. "First you're going to wash up, and have some breakfast. That will make you feel better."

"Will it?"

"Trust me. Routine is very soothing to the psyche." When she saw the subtle, dour twist of his lips, she became more determined. "Excuse me, Mr. Pessimist. But I learned that from watching animals. You can set clocks by some. I think part of it's due to the fact that their world is very uncertain. They use patterns and rituals to cut down on stress."

She retrieved the towel she'd spread on the rattan chair nearby and handed it to him. "So up and at 'em."

He didn't budge.

"Do you need help?" Then it struck her. She broke into a cheeky grin. "Why, darling, modesty? After the night we shared?'' She watched him rack his brain for a clue. Wanting only to get his mind off his worries, not tease him cruelly, she jumped to her feet and headed for the door. "Okay, I'll let you off the hook, but call if you have a problem."

She returned to the kitchen regretting that she hadn't been the first one to wake up. "It's just my fate to look like the aftereffects of a tornado no matter when he sees me," she muttered, checking her reflection in the kitchen stove.

But as usual, she wasted little time on self-pity, or regrets. Smelling the fresh coffee, she poured herself a mug and focused on getting somewhat organized.

There was plenty to do before he reappeared. First she opened Honey's cage to let her fly about a bit if she chose, while Dr. J. was out.

Honey always chose. She landed on Frankie's shoulder with a kamikaze shriek. "*Erk.* Grape . . . grape."

"Why is it that the first and last word out of your mouth every day is always about food?"

"Who loves ya, baby?"

"Too little, too late."

But she grinned as she headed back to the kitchen. Usually it was a toss-up as to who would reach her shoulder first, the red-and-blue parrot or her iguana. Mealtime brought out the theatrics in the group, as much as the athletics; but because she had an added responsibility today, she was altering her schedule somewhat and throwing everyone else off.

So, despite a scampering sound as she passed the bookcase by the door, Bugsy didn't try to bully Honey off her shoulder. It was late, and all he cared about was food, too.

"Grape. Gimmee . . . gimmee."

"Hold your horses." Frankie took another sip of coffee before uncovering a bowl of fruit on the counter. She barely had a berry between her fingers before the parrot snatched it.

"That was Bugsy's, young lady. Okay, Bugs, here you go," she then said, lifting another grape up to where he perched. His cavernous mouth opened and she dropped in the peridot green fruit that was almost a perfect match to the lizard's scaly skin.

From outside came a low, annoyed whine, followed by a raking sound against the screen. Frankie glanced back to see Dr. J. glaring at her with Callie as his ally.

"I did not trick you into going out so I wouldn't have to feed you. I'll open a can of tuna as soon as I get our new friend's sausage cooking."

She knew Dr. J. and Callie would have preferred one of the fresh fish Mr. Miller had brought yesterday, but she needed time to cook them. The stump-tailed gray cat would cost her a small fortune, if it wasn't for Mr. Miller's kind attention and generosity.

Stretch was the only one she didn't have to worry about this morning. He'd eaten well yesterday, and wouldn't need more for another day or two.

Still, that left her with a yard full of noisy, hungry animals. Quite a racket when you weren't used to it. Out of compassion for her guest's aching head, Frankie quickly finished feeding Honey and Bugsy, and hurried out to toss a few treats to the others to tide them over—dog biscuits to Maury and Samson, an apple to Rasputin and Lambchop, a bit of shredded chicken breast to Dr. J. and Callie. George still had some grain from yesterday, so she gratefully sprinted back inside to wash her hands, and get back to her patient.

She had the Silver Duck smelling of sausage and hash browns by the time she heard the bathroom door open. She looked up from spreading margarine on the toast, surprised when her guest appeared wearing a green terry robe instead of the expected towel.

"Is it okay to borrow this?"

She found his tentative, almost-shy look appealing. "My goodness . . . well, sure. I forgot all about it. That belonged to my grandfather. I keep it because in cooler weather it's wonderful to snuggle in. But isn't it a bit warm for you?"

"That's okay."

It had fit her grandfather perfectly, but on the stranger it was considerably short in the sleeves and length; however, she didn't have to be a mind reader to figure out that hot or not, it made him feel a great deal more comfortable than wearing the towel.

As he approached her, he eyed with caution the group at the screen door and then the parrot, who sat on the back of one of the bar stools. "I thought I dreamed them."

"Wishful thinking, huh?"

"No, they..." Finally noting her teasing smile, he ducked his head and eyed her from beneath board-straight eyebrows. "Maybe a little. Where's the snake?"

"Under the couch. He'll probably stay there hoping to get back in my good graces, so I'll let him play in the shower."

His answering look suggested he didn't know whether to take her seriously or not. "Do any of them bite?"

She didn't want to cross her fingers behind her back again, and answered with diplomatic care. "Probably not. They're usually all very loving and grateful to have a home."

"Probably? Usually?"

Apparently he was sharp even when suffering from a lumpy head and amnesia. Frankie abandoned her strategy with an easygoing shrug. "What good would my guarantee be if one decided he didn't like the way you moved or sounded, and nipped you on the leg or finger? I never know how they'll react to company."

He didn't take his eyes off her. "Do you get much?"

What an odd question. She wouldn't flatter herself by accepting the first reason for it that came to mind, but she refused to consider the second. Not after he'd been a perfect gentleman last night. Rarely. "Well, there's Mr. Miller. He's my landlord, so to speak, and a real dear. So sometimes he'll drop by to fish for me or bring some from the pond near his house. I can't bear to kill and clean the little guys myself."

"I don't think I know him."

His face took on an irresistible charm when touched by anxiety or confusion. It broke Frankie's heart not to be able to be more assuring. "I don't think so, either." She told him about the widower's problem with poachers after losing the helper who'd resided at this corner of the ranch. "In return for having the use of this trailer site, I keep an eye on the place and his cattle when they're rotated to this southernmost pasture."

"More animals."

Frankie didn't find his fatalistic comment reassuring. "Cows. They *are* fenced. Don't you like animals?"

He fisted his hands by his side. "I don't know. Everything you've said so far, this whole scenario feels like something out of *Alice in Wonderland*."

"Forget it then and come sit down." Not wanting to upset him further, Frankie beckoned him the bar stool beside Honey. "Do you like— Have some of this cranberry juice I just poured," she amended, silently chastising herself for almost blundering again. "I hope you're hungry, because I may have overdone it with the food. But you look like you need a lot to fill up."

"I am hungry." He eased onto the swivel chair, only to glance over his shoulder at the protest from beyond the screen door.

"Ignore Dr. J. You just happen to be sitting in his favorite chair."

Her guest scratched his eyebrow slowly. "Let me guess.... He likes to play basketball?"

"With the parrot as the ball. That's why these hands will never be used in jewelry ads." She wiggled her fingers, indicating new scratches and healing scars, before returning to the task of scooping the scrambled eggs onto his plate.

A soft braying sound and a patient bark had her pointing with her spatula toward the screen door where some of the others were collecting, drawn by the sound of her voice. "The goat is Rasputin, who you may recall tried to turn your blanket into a snack last night."

"I think I remember a hoof on my foot, but I thought it was all delusionary. Why Rasputin?"

"Look at that black face, those intense eyes, and those wild eyebrows and beard, then tell me if you can think of a better name for him. Maury is the German shepherd. You'll want to approach him from the front or right side, because he's blind in his left eye."

"Maybe I'll pass on approaching him at all. He's huge."

"You should try lifting him into the community bathtub, but he's a pussycat—speaking of which, the little calico is Callie."

"I remember her. The first time I thought I was losing my mind was seeing her staring at me through the windshield."

"She may only have three legs, but you'll find she manages as well as any feline at her age."

"How many, er, pets are there in all?"

"Ten at the moment. The number changes depending on who I can find a good home for, and who passes on due to injuries or old age. It gets a bit tough sometimes."

"You have a soft heart," he murmured, his gaze sober again. "Probably too soft."

Here he was, dealing with amnesia and who knew what else, and he was concerned for her? "Someone has to help them. And when you're dealing with anything having to do with nature and life, it's inevitable that there are going to be low moments. But the rewards outweigh the sad or painful times." She set his plate before him. "Now, enough philosophizing. Eat."

He didn't have to be told twice. Shaky though his hands were, he attacked his food with a zest that made Frankie wonder when he'd last had a meal. She wasn't about to make the mistake of asking, though. Let him have at least a few moments to dine in peace. Instead she began opening cans of pet food and scooping up rations of dry cereal for her animal family.

"You're not eating?"

She indicated the toast-wrapped sausage she'd already taken a bite of. "I don't need much to keep me going. Oops..." Remembering the coffee, she interrupted the other task to pour him a mugful. "Let's try black," she said, setting it before him.

With a murmured "Thanks," he sipped the brew, and his cautious expression quickly ripened into full, sensual pleasure. "Mmm. Good. I think I drink it this way."

She felt as pleased for him as if he'd just remembered his social security number. "There, you see? Progress already!"

He took another drink before setting down the mug and picking up his fork again. A frown formed between his eyebrows, and although Frankie thought it gave him a somewhat intellectual, wholly sexy look, she wondered what she'd triggered now.

"Tell me about where you found me," he said quietly.

"Wouldn't you rather eat in peace? We can talk afterward."

"Avoiding the issue isn't going to make my problem go away. I need to get some answers. There are so many blank spaces in my head, I feel like one big... black hole. Do you have any idea what that's like?"

No, and what's more, she didn't want to think about him enduring that. But she had already ascertained that when she talked, he gave her his full attention, and right now he needed to feed his body instead of his mind.

"Let me at least get the animals taken care of." And she darned well intended to spruce up herself, too. Before he could either protest or agree, she lifted the loaded tray of cans, measuring cups of cereal, apples and carrots, and hurried for the door. "It won't take long," she said, nudging the screen open with her hip.

She had her routine streamlined for efficiency and fine-tuned to a nutritional science. That didn't mean her furry friends didn't provide a challenge or two. Callie insisted on checking out everyone's food before agreeing to settle on hers, which could create jealousy and some fulfilled threats. Lambchop didn't understand her disproportionate size to the others and thought she should be able to eat hers from the deck like everyone else—even if that meant stepping in Frankie's small but cherished flower bed.

"Lambchop—doggone it! I guess I'm just not supposed to have flowers like normal people," she muttered, once she spotted the crushed blossoms beneath the donkey's club-foot. "I find the one variety of bloom that Rasputin and Samson won't devour, and you have to mash my marigolds into papyrus."

When it came to beautifying herself, Frankie had to forget about any personal pampering and settle for a quick face scrubbing and tooth brushing. Her hair was a hopeless case, too, due to southeast Texas's humid environment. What encouraged forests to grow lush, and flowers to explode with color, turned her long blond hair into a wild mass of curls that resisted any form of control no matter how often and long she brushed it. There was no time to even try today.

With a shrug, she loosely braided it, the results a far cry from glamour, unless the hippie look was back in style. "Well, Park Avenue chic was never you, anyway, remember?" she told her reflection with a meaningful look of rebuke. "Lordy, a sexy man shows up, and you start getting all these wild ideas. What's next? Makeup?"

"Frankie... *Frankie!*"

She'd actually been reaching for the mascara she used for work because the sun bleached her lashes. With a sigh, she shut the catchall drawer and ran to see what had put that note of stress in the stranger's voice. As if she didn't have at least a small clue...

"Bugsy! You don't eat potatoes!"

The reptile had ventured from his secret hideaway and was checking out what remained of her guest's breakfast. Frankie picked him up and carted him outside to the caged area she'd created for him. There he would be able to watch the others while not getting hurt or lost.

"If you're still hungry, find yourself a nice juicy bug or two," she told him, securing the cage's door.

Upon her return, she gave the stranger an apologetic smile.

"Sorry about that. Um... he's number ten. He's an iguana."

"You sleep with a boa, a bobcat, and an iguana?"

She could tell by his expression that if she told him she swallowed fire, too, he wouldn't be any more surprised. "I don't actually *sleep* with them. Well, Dr. J. does like extra body heat in the winter, but he's a Manx, not a bobcat. A customer at The Two-Step was moving overseas and asked me to take him in. Bugsy joined us when I saved him from becoming an appetizer at a rather strange restaurant in California.''

As she spoke, Frankie dashed around the counter to refill their mugs, then dashed back to sit down on the stool that Honey had abandoned for the windowsill by the sink.

"Okay. I'm ready to talk if you are."

The stranger blinked as if dealing with a sudden attack of vertigo. Frankie sympathized, aware that she sometimes had the same effect on people even when they weren't suffering from head trauma.

"I don't think I've ever met anyone quite like you before," he ventured slowly.

"You're probably right."

"Give me a minute to— You mentioned Houston. Are we near Houston?"

"About a two-hour drive north. That's due to traffic, not actual distance. This area is known as Slocum Springs. Does that ring any bells?" When he didn't respond, she added, "How about Dallas? Texas? The United States of America?"

One glance at his pained features, and she regretted the droll remark. Sometimes she indulged in just too much impish humor. She needed to respect that as bizarre as the situation was to her, it had to be terrifying to him.

She reached over and touched his arm. "I'm sorry. I wish I had the power to make you wake up and realize you'd only had a bad dream."

"So do I," he murmured, raising his gaze from her hand to search her face. "Except that would mean you weren't real."

Just when she thought she had control of her fanciful mind, he had to say something like that, his eyes had to turn that darker, smoky color that emphasized his seriousness, and intimacy. Afraid she would do something completely stupid, Frankie returned to the protection of humor.

"Let me tell you, there are more than a few people who wish I *was* a figment of their imagination."

"I don't believe that."

He had the nicest voice. Mild and smooth, but at the same time utterly masculine. Frankie sighed. "I wish I knew if you always found it easy to talk to women."

"I doubt it."

"Why?"

"Because whatever I say to you feels too right."

It did to her, too. That was the wonder of it, and at the same time what concerned her. In fact, she suddenly knew that if he would ask her this minute to—

He abruptly turned back to the counter and clasped his hands around his mug. "You better not look at me that way."

"Why?"

"Well, I've been thinking about it and...for all you know, I'm a wanted felon, or worse."

She found it easy to jump to his defense. "You can't believe that!" Back in the beginning the idea had crossed her mind, as well, but she couldn't accept it.

"We can't discount that it's a possibility. Especially since... Frankie, as frightening as it is to have nothing but questions, I'm not sure I want to find out the truth."

"But the truth could ease your mind!"

"I know you must think I'm nuts, and I'm not sure I can explain it. When I try to think of my life, I feel this dread. Maybe I was just unhappy before. Maybe I was making someone else unhappy and this is residual guilt I'm dealing with. Or maybe it's more serious and I'm a bad person," he continued, his voice growing gruff. "Maybe I've escaped from prison or some institution. Wherever I came from, whoever I am, try as I might, I can't pick up any images. The harder I try, the darker my vision gets, and the more difficult it is to breathe. It's a relief to leave it alone."

"You're relieved that you're alive. Someone obviously meant to harm you—permanently." Contrary to what her family believed, there were times when she wouldn't let the dreamer inside her have too much control, and this was one of them. Frankie put down her own coffee and leaned toward him. "But what if you are a good person? What if you have an entire life somewhere, with people, *children* waiting for you?"

He started shaking his head before she'd finished. Like his expression, his tone was adamant. "It's not possible."

"Why?"

"Because it's not. I don't feel it. Nothing."

"That doesn't mean they don't exist."

"Oh, God..." He lifted his hands to either side of his head. "My head's going to explode."

Despite what he'd told her about his darkest fears, Frankie came straight out of her chair and put her arms around him.

"All right. Shh... All right, try to relax, don't fight it. You'll just make it worse. Shh..."

She stroked his back and when he wrapped his arms around her and pressed his head against her breasts, his trembling became hers. His torment and anguish, too. As she smoothed his hair, she already knew that wise or not, she would have to be a harder, colder person to turn away from this man and his need.

"Frankie, will you help me?"

The way he'd had to force that question past his stiff lips told her that he hadn't asked for help very often in his life. She swallowed the lump that lodged in her throat, and lowered her cheek to the top of his head. "Yes. I'll help."

Once she voiced her decision, she felt a wave of peace permeate the room. No matter what happened, what it cost her, she knew she'd done a necessary thing. Her instincts to protect, to provide a corner of sanctuary in a chaotic, brutal world had surfaced with every one of the animals who'd ever come into her care, but never this strongly. This was right.

"That's it? No more arguments? Protests?"

"There are plenty of both, but no. I won't make them now."

"You'll let me stay?"

"For a while. Until you decide otherwise." *Or change your mind... or remember...*

"Why?" he asked, gazing up at her.

"Beats me." It was okay to tease again. Gently. She wouldn't let the anguish remain in the depths of his eyes for long. Such a face as his was meant for sunshine and laughter. Something told her that he didn't indulge in enough of either.

Expecting somber words of gratitude, she was stunned when he pressed a kiss between her breasts and murmured his thanks.

Frankie's breath locked in her throat. Fissions of sweet, hot desire shot through her body faster than that bolt of lightning that had split Mr. Miller's oak in the pasture last spring. She ached for him to do it again, to shift slightly and brush his lips across her breast, take her into his mouth. Her nipples grew painfully hard from the need, and she could feel his body's sudden strong arousal, too.

Shocked at how quickly things had altered between them, she could only stare down at his brown hair in wonder, and more than a little concern.

"We can't— This isn't wise," she managed, although her voice was reed thin.

"I know," he replied against her thrumming heart. "But you feel . . . like home."

He did, too, that was the problem. She grasped at some link to sanity. "I don't even know what to call you!"

After a second, he sighed and glanced up at her. "What do you want to call me? I'll answer to anything. How about Fido?"

Crazy, endearing man. Frankie didn't bother trying to stop the incredulous laughter that bubbled from inside her, thinking that he might not like that she was already beginning to rub off on him. "It has potential, but I think I'll save it for someone with four legs." Another somewhat wicked idea came to mind.

Francesca Rose Jones, you can't!

"How about Johnny?" she heard herself suggest. As soon as she spoke, however, she groaned and shook her head. "No, never mind, it's a dumb idea. Forget it."

He frowned slightly, then fixed his dark blue and suddenly savvy, eyes on her. "I get it. Frankie and Johnny. That's from a song, right?"

"Yes, but it was a movie that came to mind." She could tell he had never seen it—or had he? She had only to meet his penetrating gaze and she remembered the unexpected, steamy sensuality between Al Pacino and Michelle Pfeiffer.

"They were lovers."

"Yes, but I didn't mean to suggest . . ."

"I know."

"Because we can't."

"I know." He sighed as if pulling out a long thorn from his flesh. "But in here—" he took her hand and placed it against his chest "—we already are. Lovers."

It was true. She'd known it last night, only she'd tried to pretend otherwise, and she could feel it in his heartbeat now, which felt like a sledgehammer about to come through

Sheetrock. "I won't let myself hurt anyone," she said, struggling for the tiniest hold on sanity by thinking of his possible ties elsewhere.

"We won't."

"And you have to accept that one day you'll remember. You'll want to leave." Or have to.

"No one ever knows how long they have."

That was crazy. An invitation to heartbreak.

He took her hand again, moved it in a slow circle around his heart. "Say it, Frankie. Say my name."

He made her want to cry. He made her want to run. But most of all he made her ache for what she knew—what they both seemed to know—could be . . . if fate decided to be benevolent and kind. Dare she hope? Dare she believe in the magic his eyes and touch promised?

Finders keepers . . . finders keepers . . .

Oh, to be so lucky.

"Frankie . . . ?"

She drew a deep breath, and smiled in welcome. "Hello, Johnny."

Four

After such an emotional exchange, Frankie insisted Johnny had drained himself enough, and that he needed to go back to bed, if only to lie down for a while. He went, albeit grumbling, and to her amusement fell asleep almost immediately.

The respite gave her a much-needed chance to get used to the idea that she'd taken on what would amount to being the most difficult challenge of her life. It again brought on the thought that if she had nails, she would have bitten them to nubs, but yard work and caring for her animals had settled that matter long ago. Besides, the nail-biting wouldn't have burned the adrenaline racing inside her.

After taking care of the breakfast dishes, she resorted to doing some of those never-ending chores. When she had company, she verbalized her thoughts to her animals.

"Do you think I've lost my mind this time, Lambchop?" she asked the donkey, while treating her to a late-morning brushing in the shade. "Never mind. It doesn't matter anyway, because it's a done deal. I said yes. Now I'm committed to helping him."

Several minutes later, she was filling the community water trough and brooding about what her decision meant. "After all, it's one thing to have let you guys move in," she said to Maury, as he joined her to lap at the fresh well-water. Like the others, he preferred drinking it to pond water, although the pond was fed by a creek. "At least I didn't have to think up a history for you.

"He'll need a last name and everything," she told Samson, as she sprayed the pig's personal mud puddle. "And what about clothes? How am I supposed to figure out what size he wears? Ask him? That'll be a hoot."

A bark behind her had her spinning around. She always talked to them, but it was a bit embarrassing to be caught doing it by a third party. Not just any third party. *This* one in particular.

Johnny stepped off the deck and cautiously petted Maury before joining her. "Do they answer?"

She wrinkled her nose at him. "It would serve you right if I said yes. Then you'd really think you were in some other world." Her grin turned into a frown and she pointed downward. "You shouldn't be out here barefoot. You can't afford to risk a bee or scorpion sting. What do I say if I have to take you to a hospital, after all, and they ask if you're allergic to anything or not?"

A heat-loving bullfrog croaked by the pond. Way above, a hawk called as it scanned the ground for a field mouse or mole. The sounds were intense in the subsequent silence, and so was his lengthy perusal.

"Are you regretting your decision to let me stay?" he asked at last.

Frankie shut off the water, but delayed answering him. Before she could wind the hose back onto its holder by the faucet, Johnny took it from her and did it himself. Then he took her hand and led her to the porch steps.

"Come sit with me here. The sun feels good."

"As pale as you are, you can't afford being out in it too much."

"You are feeling grouchy." He didn't look as though it bothered him at all. "You should have taken a nap with me."

Oh, that would have been smart.

"Come on, tell me. What's wrong?"

"Nothing, really. Just a bunch of little concerns that one by one don't amount to much, but as a whole... Forget it. You'd just think I'm crazy."

"I *think* you're wonderful. Nothing's changed."

No, something had. She'd made him a promise. She knew his body almost as well as he did. He'd touched her in a place most of her dates had never reached. They were intimate strangers who now had to write their own rule book about what that meant and how to deal with it.

But dealing with his company was easy. They settled just out of reach of the shady loblolly pine tree that draped over the deck and part of the trailer and the July sun was baking a clay ground that hadn't seen rain in a week. But Frankie didn't notice anything except Johnny's appreciation of the rays beating down on him.

"How do you feel?" For someone who'd fallen asleep so quickly, he still looked drawn and tense. "Did those aspirin I gave you work?"

"Somewhat." He looked around the pasture, the pond, the strip of woods that separated this eastern pasture from the western one, as if eager to change the subject. "This is a nice place. I was watching you for a few minutes after I woke, and—"

"You were! Why?"

"Because it's impossible not to. You're like a daffodil in the sun—full of life, no matter what you're doing. Beautiful."

She'd been called cute before, and perky, even pretty. But never had she been called beautiful. More important, never had she wanted to believe such a compliment.

Afraid of the depth of her feelings, Frankie redirected their conversation again. "Well, since you're awake now, I should go in and change. I'm going to have to leave for a while to get you some clothes before I head for work."

"I'm already causing trouble for you, aren't I?"

"It's all right. Do you think you can manage here by yourself?"

"I hope so. I'd better."

True, if he really meant it about staying. "If someone should come by..." she continued, thinking of potential problems.

"Are you expecting anyone to?"

"Not at this hour. Mr. Miller usually brings over any mail there might be in the mornings, but my family has his telephone number, too, in case of an emergency."

"You don't have a phone?"

It pleased her that he didn't know. She told herself that it meant he hadn't checked, that he wasn't sneaky. "Nope. It would be a waste."

"You don't miss talking to your family?"

"I told you, I'm the black sheep. Why call to hear everything you're doing wrong with your life? I write. They write—some of them. It's enough." How on earth had they gotten off track? "In any case, I was thinking about how to explain your presence if someone did drop by."

"I could be a friend. A close friend," he amended wryly, glancing down at the robe.

"A friend from school."

"You said you didn't go to school."

"I didn't graduate. High school, then."

"We've kept in touch all these years?"

"Wouldn't you have?" she asked, suddenly intrigued with the way this conversation was going.

"Yes. But if I'd written . . ."

"Ah, a hole in our logic. With Mr. Miller seeing my mail that would trigger questions. Good point. I guess I need to work on lying."

"I'm glad you're not good at it." He fingered the end of her braid resting over her left shoulder. "Why don't you tell me who has been in your life. Maybe that will give us an idea."

Maybe this was a sneaky way to learn about her love life. "There were only two," she said, shrugging because there was nothing to hide. "Andy made it clear early on that he was looking for a rich wife, and found her in the form of an up-and-coming investment consultant. Ted stole from me and then lied about it. I guess I do better with animals."

"How long since Ted?"

"Just over a year and a half."

"Then I'll be number three."

"But everyone knows I'm not looking for number three."

"You think fate waits until you're ready?"

He spoke so softly, Frankie almost believed she'd imagined the question. She stared at him with new respect—and concern. "I'm beginning to think you may be a natural at this."

"No. You make it easy." This time he picked up her braid and caressed her cheek with the silky end. "You give temptation a new name, Frankie."

She didn't know what to say. She knew what she *wanted* to say, do. She wanted to wrap her arms around his neck and let him whisper sweet nothings to her until the moon came up, then start all over again. Learn how he kissed. Learn what pleased him.

The braid moved to her lip. Either it or he was reading her mind . . . or her expression.

"So what's my last name and where did we meet?"

"How about . . . Ash? Like your hair."

"Johnny Ash." He raised a hand to his head as if only just realizing the color. "I don't know."

As if seconding his lack of enthusiasm, Maury rolled over and indulged in a big, lazy yawn. Frankie sat up. "Oh, thank you, Maury! How about Shepherd?"

"Shepherd. John Shepherd. That feels better." Johnny nodded toward the dog. "Do I claim him as a distant cousin?"

"Very distant," Frankie replied, with an equally straight face.

"Where did we meet? You and I, that is."

"How about . . . Dallas. It was a hot summer day. You were the taxicab driver who helped me change a flat tire on the trailer." Mischief got the best of her again. "It was dust at first sight."

Johnny's lips curved. His wonderful eyes came close to twinkling. "Has anyone ever told you that you have the most unexpected sense of humor?"

Not at the moment. At the moment her thoughts were torpedoing her spirits.

"The only problem," she said as if he hadn't spoken, "is that you don't have a Texas accent."

"I don't?" He, too, grew somber. "I don't."

She hated seeing the shadows return to his eyes. "I'm sorry." This had been such fun.

"There's no avoiding it. No matter what we talk about, it's going to hit us right in the face, over and over."

Frankie struggled to think of a history for him that would be comfortable for them both. "What if you are that old school chum, but you'd been traveling and we'd lost track of each other. When you returned to Pennsylvania, you got in touch with me through my parents."

He eyed her dubiously. "How old are you, Frankie?"

"Twenty-seven."

"How old do I look?" He gestured to his face. "Even without these bruises I figure I'm several years older, minimum. Would *you* believe we were school buddies?"

"Then let's tell the truth. I'll say we met when I almost ran you down. We won't say where or when. We'll just be vague."

"I can do that without trying."

Frankie touched a finger to his lips. "Stop beating yourself up."

Johnny took hold of her hand. "So small. I haven't thought enough about how much responsibility I'm heaping on you. I hope I'm worth it, Frankie."

"You have to believe you are. I do."

"Make sure. Make sure you take something for yourself, too. Be selfish for once. I won't mind."

She couldn't have responded if she'd wanted to. She understood what he meant, what he was offering.

His fingers tightened, as his gaze shifted to her mouth. "On second thought you'd better—I think you'd better go do that shopping, or I'm going to break my word to myself about not touching you."

He was giving her a chance to escape, but Frankie couldn't make herself move. "You are touching me."

It seemed an eternity until he closed the distance between them and brushed his lips against hers. When it happened,

Frankie stopped breathing, too caught up in the sensations; the warm and exciting and so, so sweet sensations. Yielding to them, Frankie felt something unfold and blossom inside her.

Then he kissed her again. And again.

She didn't know how it happened; how, between the second and third kiss, the tender emotions between them transformed into something entirely different. But as impossible as it seemed, it happened. One moment she felt absolutely cherished, and the next she felt she was cresting the highest peak of a roller coaster, about to plunge into somewhere wild and uncontrollable.

It took all her willpower to jerk back. The way Johnny uttered her name spoke of his own shock. She heard him as she scrambled to her feet and rushed inside.

What are you doing, Jonesy, asking for a broken heart on top of who knows what else?

Feeling more than a little vulnerable and painfully raw around the edges, she knew the smartest thing would be to put more distance between them, and so she quickly washed up and changed into the lavender T-shirt and jeans she would wear to work later on.

When she returned outside, she found that Johnny hadn't budged from his seat on the steps. He was, however, bracing his head on his folded hands like a man in pain, or prayer.

"I guess I'd better be going."

He exhaled and sat up. "I owe you another apology. I got carried away."

"You had help. We're adults, Johnny. We understand chemistry and stress. No permanent damage done." This time, she thought. "I'll be back as soon as I can."

He nodded, but didn't turn around. Murmuring a barely audible, "Goodbye," Frankie hurried for Petunia, never more aware of his eyes following her.

Adult. You're an adult. The thought twisted into a taunt minutes later, as Johnny removed his bandage and studied his reflection in the bathroom mirror. He sure looked old enough to know better. With that ugly bruise turning nastier shades of blue and purple, plus the deepening lines in his face, he could pass for forty and felt like he was going on fifty. But his mind... Hell, the lack of personal history in his memory banks made him feel like a newborn. Worse, a simpleton.

"A damned blank page," he muttered, bending to splash more water on his face. And at this point, nightmares would be more welcome than having to deal with guilt over what had happened between him and Frankie. Not even the headache that was back in full force, seemed like adequate punishment; nor did it stop the hunger.

But sore as he was, he remained hot and needy. Because she'd been so good to hold, to kiss. He wished he could remember if it was because it had been a long time since he'd made love. He had a hunch he already knew the answer to that: it was her.

"Frankie."

He reached for a towel to dry off, and the mere taste of her name on his tongue stirred the passion throbbing inside him. She was part child, part angel, but first and foremost, a woman. In less than twenty-four hours she'd both stunned him with her kindness, and made him plead for her continued generosity; but after only one taste of her, he was ready to risk it all to beg her to make love with him.

What was he doing to her? To *them*? Promises aside, how could he be sure he wouldn't hurt her? Last night she'd treated him like a homeless pup looking for a free meal and a snug place to sleep. That proved she had the survival instincts of a moth. What if he'd been an escaped con, or a rapist or serial killer?

Who says you're not?

As a shaft of fierce pain speared through his head, he swore and stumbled out of the bathroom. He needed to lie down again. Just for a few minutes. He wasn't sleepy or anything; it was the damn dizziness and nausea that came even when he tried to think about what had happened last night in those last moments before Frankie found him.

Clearly his spared life and Frankie were gifts. "Don't blow it," he muttered, as he sought a comfortable position on the pillow. With a sigh he closed his eyes.

It would have been faster to go to another store. She could have gone in a different direction to get to Fair Mart. But no sooner did she leave home than Frankie knew she had to return to the spot near the interstate to see if she could locate something that might identify Johnny, or maybe even help him get his memory back.

She could have called what she was doing panic; on the other hand, some would say it was simply insurance. Both labels worked, if she'd been the type to believe in labels. Cynical. But she was simply functioning in her usual mode—life by the seat of her pants. Instincts.

The idea to return to where she'd found Johnny had crossed her mind and stayed. Ideas that stayed usually meant something.

On her way, she only slowed down and scanned the place, pinpointing where she thought she saw a trace of Petunia's eternal oil leak on the gravel shoulder. In daylight the area looked like any country roadway in southeastern Texas— green, lush, and heavily wooded by pine and hardwood trees. Mostly pine, though, because they were close to the Davey Crockett State Park. Serious timber country as the locals called it with pride. The pride turned to dread once the dry heat of summer brought on one forest fire after another. But it had only been dry in the past week or so; everything could still be called "juicy" green, as she'd heard one of Mr. Miller's grandchildren describe it. Ironically, that didn't necessarily present good news for her.

With a lesser threat of fire, the county road departments had been a bit more lax with their mowing schedule. They hadn't cut the county-road easements since the spring wildflowers had gone to seed back in May. They wouldn't mow again until late next month, or in early September. Frankie had driven on to the store aware that she would be the picnic if she trod through the knee-high vegetation.

About an hour later, she stepped cautiously through the tall grass. Well beyond where she'd looked last night. She was glad for her jeans and jogging shoes, and that she'd bought a can of insect repellent at Fair Mart. She'd sprayed her clothes from the knees down against the chiggers that would make a mosquito bite feel like a love pat. If something larger lurked... Well, she refused to dwell on that, having enough on her mind between hoping she would find something, and hoping she wouldn't.

She played a game with herself. Look for five minutes, she stipulated. Go no farther than the utility pole. Chances are he hadn't been beyond that point, either. If she didn't come across anything, it would be a sign for her to quit and go home. It would mean she'd been meant to help Johnny last night.

Finders keepers.

She needn't tell him. Why upset him unnecessarily?

Unless she found something.

Depending on what she found.

What if it means doing something morally or legally wrong?

That proved one question too many.

She started back to Petunia, pleased at least that not one vehicle had passed during her search. However, no sooner did she mentally pat herself on the back, than a state trooper's black-and-white pulled up behind her truck.

"Nothing like tempting trouble," she whispered between stiff lips.

The cop eased from the car and adjusted the wide brim of his hat as he eyed her over the white roof. He didn't offer a smile and she couldn't begin to guess what message his eyes relayed behind his sunglasses.

"Trouble, ma'am?"

"Uh—no, officer. I was going shopping a while ago and I lost something. I thought I'd stop on my way home and see if maybe it landed over here."

"What did you lose?"

Now what are you going to say, Miss Brilliant?

"My... an earring." As she approached the officer, she did a brief but busy pantomime to indicate her bare lobe, her hair, which had, indeed, come loose from the braid in the wind, and the fact that it had been tugged off. Was she convincing, though?

"Was it an expensive piece? That's a fairly snaky area, and this location is a bit remote for a lady to be wandering around by herself."

"You know, I'd just come to that conclusion myself. And it was only costume stuff. Sentimental value," she said, stopping on the other side of his patrol car, "but not worth taking unnecessary risks over. Thank you, officer."

"Do you live near here?"

"A few miles east on the Miller farm. I work at The Two-Step." She pointed in both directions in case he wasn't that familiar with the area. "Do you need to see my license?"

"What for?"

Frankie could have groaned for that one. Next she would be sticking out her hands, inviting him to slap handcuffs on her wrists.

"Just checking. I thought it was routine. Well, I have to get home and get ready for work. I appreciate the advice and your concern."

"Be careful."

Did he see her sweating so badly that her T-shirt was sticking to her back? The way moisture was trickling along her spine, she had to wonder. And what did it mean that the officer hadn't been more curious about *where* she'd stopped? Had no one filed a missing person's report on Johnny? Did no one know where to begin looking for him?

What did that mean? Where had he come from? Where had he been going? Who had hurt him? Had they meant to kill him? Did that mean they might try again if they found out they'd been unsuccessful?

The questions came fast and furiously, and as Frankie pulled away from the officer, she knew they wouldn't stop until she had some answers. The only way to do that without alarming Johnny, or putting Petunia in reverse and telling the trooper the truth, would be to check the news on TV later when she arrived at the club.

Her decision made, Frankie returned home relieved that things hadn't gotten complicated with the state trooper. As she pulled into the yard, only Samson, ever hungry, came to greet her. The rest stayed in their pockets of shade, too hot and lazy to budge. She was relieved, since she had quite a load to carry and didn't need a bunch of noses and drooling mouths slowing her progress. There wasn't, however, any sign of the beneficiary of her bounty.

"Johnny?" she called, entering the trailer.

Honey sat in her cage grooming herself. Bugsy now reigned over the kitchen window, nestling between the herb pots to soak in the last of the sunshine and whatever breeze came through an open window. She didn't see Stretch, which had her hurrying straight to the back in case Johnny had attempted to lie down again, only to be harassed by her snake.

She was relieved to find that wasn't the case; but what did disturb her, was seeing Johnny. He was writhing and moaning, clearly caught in the throes of a bad dream.

Dumping her armload of bags on the far side of the bed, she circled back to try to wake him. "Johnny?" With the first touch she knew he was burning with fever. "Johnny, wake up. You're—oh!"

Before she could finish her sentence, he'd whipped around and gripped her wrists in a bone-breaking hold. The look in his eyes was feral.

"Johnny, please!"

"Frankie!"

"It's me. You were having a bad dream, but you're all right now."

Dazed, glassy eyes stared up at her blankly for several seconds before he relaxed his hold. "Frankie," he rasped, sinking back into the pillow.

His relief was almost a tangible thing, and her heart went out to him. He'd also ripped off his bandage in his sleep and had reopened the wound a bit. She couldn't see where the gauze and bandages were, but the scene was so disconcerting, she hardly paid attention that all his tossing and turning had left him virtually naked again.

"Let me get something. You're sweating like crazy and bleeding again. I'll be right back."

By the time she returned, he was sitting up on the side of the bed and had recovered enough to tug the robe back on. "Damn it, Frankie..." he muttered, gesturing to the bloody sheets. "I'm sorry. What a mess."

"Don't worry about it. It'll come out. Drink this." She had a bowl of cold water and a washcloth, and had a bottle of cold water from the refrigerator for him to drink.

While he quenched his considerable thirst, she dabbed at the new stream of blood still trickling from his forehead. Once it slowed, she rinsed the washcloth and mopped at his perspiring face and throat.

"Better?" she asked, when he signaled he'd had enough to drink. She took the bottle from him and set it on the table.

"Much, but what about you? Did I hurt you?"

"Nothing's broken."

"That's not funny."

She dismissed his protest to focus on something else. "Tell me about the dream you were having. Do you remember any of it?"

He avoided her gaze. "Not to the point where it made any sense."

"You want to tell me? Sometimes that helps."

With a moan, he closed his eyes. "The darkness was more pronounced this time. I was thrown into darkness ... into a box."

"Do you think that's how you got hurt?"

"No, I—" He frowned. "It doesn't make any sense."

"What doesn't?"

"The dream. What I saw."

"And what was that?"

"Someone else because it couldn't have been me. It was a kid! Ten...maybe twelve years old. He wasn't me. I mean I *felt* as if he was, but he wasn't. How could that be?"

He'd posed a good question. Although she wouldn't begin to pretend she understood the intricacies of how the mind worked, she knew it could do amazing, sometimes inexplicable things in order to cope with stress and trauma. "Maybe you needed to think this was happening to someone else, someone much younger, in order to cope, to accept you felt fear?" she suggested gently.

"Maybe." He exhaled shakily. "I sure felt like a child. Helpless. Lost."

He shuddered and Frankie sat down beside him. "What?"

"Betrayed. I also felt...betrayed and angry. Violently so."

When he shuddered again, she didn't hesitate wrapping her arms around him although his comment about violence unsettled her. "It's all right. It's over and you're safe now."

"I'm sweaty."

His self-consciousness and concern made her that more intent on helping him. "On you it works."

Her gentle teasing had the desired effect; after only one more halfhearted protest, he gave up and hugged her tightly to him. "Ah, Frankie..." He buried his face in the curve of her neck and shoulder. "What would I do without you?"

"You'd probably be getting arrested for streaking, I imagine." She heard his brief laugh and knew she was drawing him back from the grim place he'd slipped into. Glad to hear him sounding stronger, Frankie asked, "Do you remember anything else?"

"No. It seemed to go on and on, but now that I'm awake...no." His breath tickled the side of her neck. "Thank you."

"My pleasure."

It was inevitable that the mood between them would change. His hands, moving and caressing her back made her more aware; and he couldn't seem to get close enough to her. He stroked her hair and breathed in her scent, and when his lips brushed against the side of her neck, she felt a delicious tingling seep through her body.

"You smell so good. Like spring—clean and fresh. You're keeping the world sane for me, Frankie."

"Because I believe in you." She thought about her experience earlier and wished she could share it with him. But even if she thought he would understand, this wasn't the time. "Because I want you to get better."

"Because you're good," he murmured, his lips at her ear. "Good...and kind...and..."

As his mouth inched toward hers, Frankie's breath all but stopped in anticipation. Her entire body poised on the brink of new discovery. "Johnny, don't kiss me." Before he could misunderstand, she rushed on. "I want you to kiss me, but don't, because if you do, I'm gonna do something crazy and I can't do anything crazy because I have to go to work."

He did draw back, but the look he gave her left her as feverish as he'd been. "Maybe you should throw me out of here, Frankie. I can't seem to remember that any better than I can resist touching you."

The sincerity and anguish in his expression had her lifting her hand to his cheek. "Maybe that's why I can't throw you out, Johnny. No one's ever found it a problem to resist me before."

"Ah, sweetheart..." He took hold of her hand and placed an ardent kiss in her palm. "Don't tell me things like that. It puts even crazier ideas in my head than are already there."

Wishing she could take a risk and let him draw her with him back onto the twisted sheets, to slowly undress her, and coax her to yield to the hunger churning inside her, Frankie sighed. "Then we'd better change the subject, because I can't seem to keep from saying what's on my mind, either. Let me finish getting that head taken care of, and then maybe you'll feel like looking at what I found for you."

He didn't let go of her entirely, but he did look behind him—and sighed again. "Frankie, you did too much."

"Not really. The selection in rural areas is limited, so you may not like what I bought. But you needed a little of everything. I just hope my eye for measurements is halfway decent."

He did try on the clothes several minutes later, after Frankie put the new bandage on him, and he helped her change and clean the bloodied sheets. The clothes fit; impressively so. Only the jogging shoes were a bit snug, and Frankie promised to exchange them the following afternoon.

"Thanks," he murmured, as he stood before her in the light blue T-shirt and jeans. "But how on earth am I ever going to repay you? And when?"

Frankie dismissed his concern with a shake of her head. She couldn't get over how wonderful he looked in the clothes—strong, yet lean. Natural and incredibly sexy. If he'd been the type to prefer three-piece suits...well, it would have been a sign. One clearly stating they were all wrong for each other.

"Don't worry about that for now. We'll take one day at a time. Concentrate on getting better first."

Five

Her elated mood lingered, even though Frankie had to rush to prepare chef's salads for their dinner. Johnny helped wherever he could, and between the unique compatibility they were discovering they shared, and their increasing awareness of each other, time took on a charmed quality.

Inevitably, though, it was time to leave for the club, and as she drove there she couldn't help but remember Johnny's dream and what he'd said about it. Particularly when she passed that memorable spot.

Betrayed. Anger. What terrible words. She felt an intense dislike toward whoever had done that to him, and she wished he'd been able to give her more of a clue about what the dream meant. He'd experienced more than he'd admitted, she had sensed that much. It made her all the more determined to see what she could find out at The Two-Step.

Unfortunately, the club proved extra busy for a change. Even as she arrived, the parking lot had an unusual number of vehicles already there. The din inside was astonishing.

"Wish you'd get a dang phone," Benny shouted above the roar, as she walked in. "We could have used you an hour ago."

"What's up?" she asked, snatching up a drink tray and a handful of ashtrays. "Somebody celebrating winning the jackpot in the lottery?"

"Almost as good. Not only is it a Friday night, and payday, but both Texas teams are playing doubleheader ball games, and I managed to get another wide-screen TV brought in on time so we can pick up *both* channels!" He rubbed his hands together with glee. "Boy, we're going to clean up tonight."

"Wonderful." Frankie's enthusiasm fell flat, since this meant she had no hope whatsoever of convincing Benny to flip to the news.

She did, however, try to make the most of things, hoping that with such a crowd, not *everyone* was interested in baseball. Surely someone would be talking about current events, local happenings...? She kept one ear tuned throughout the evening. But she couldn't deny that a major part of her concentration was on Johnny back home.

A few of her customers noticed during commercials and teased her about it. Not everyone was amused by her preoccupied, often-dreamy state, though.

"Frankie, you just threw another aluminum beer can in with the glass!"

"Frankie! Is this the brand of beer I usually drink?"

"What the devil are you doing? Trying to torch the place?"

That last scolding came from Fern, the oldest but most patient of the cocktail waitresses, which was enough to have Frankie giving herself a mental shake. When she realized she'd thrown a still-lit cigarette into the paper trash bin, she groaned and quickly poured the remains of a beer over the smoking pile.

"Sorry," she replied with an apologetic grimace.

"What's with you tonight? If I didn't know better, I'd guess it had to do with an M-A-N, but I thought you'd sworn off them."

Realizing the evening need not be a complete loss, strategy-wise, Frankie smiled at the golden opportunity. "Now, Fern. You make it sound as if I signed a contract in blood or something."

"It should be mandatory that we all do," Cherry said, joining them at the bar. The redheaded waitress hitched a hip and rested her fist there. "Do you know what Edgar did? He came home last night with all this literature about starting an emu or ostrich ranch. I thought that was the one craze going around down here that I wouldn't have to worry about him contracting. So, who is he?" she demanded of Frankie without missing a beat.

Frankie thought about prolonging the questioning a bit, but as busy as they were, there just wasn't time. "A guy I met by accident. A nice guy. I almost ran him over with my truck, and we hit it off, and . . ." She let the rest hang in the air, hoping the suggestion would be enough. "His name's Johnny. Johnny Shepherd."

"Are you pulling my leg?" Ever one for a love story, Fern pushed her glasses up her nose and leaned closer. "Like in the movie *Frankie and Johnny?* This is a sign," she said to Cherry with a knowing nod.

"Oh, pu-leez," the bony woman replied. She fingered the numerous hair attachments that gave her a mane to rival some country singers' coiffures. "A couple million in a Swiss bank account, now *that* would be a sign. And no mother-in-law. What's he do?" she asked Frankie.

Frankie decided that what she and Johnny had discussed before would only gain her more of Cherry's sarcasm. "He's . . . between jobs at the moment."

Cherry rolled her Cleopatra eyes. "I'm surrounded by lunatics and Cinderellas. Baby girl, listen to your elder. I'd be a little more careful about who I fluttered my blue eyes at if I were you. Why, he could have been one of those four convicts that escaped out of Huntsville yesterday morning."

The roar in the club seemed to crescendo and then shrink as Frankie dealt with that blow. "Wh-what did you say?"

"It's okay now. They got the last one this evening. I heard it on the news just before I came in. But it's a good reminder to take extra care, especially how you live way out there on your own."

Relieved but rattled, Frankie watched her hoist her loaded drink tray and sashay off. How easy it would have been for Johnny to be one of those men; they were only a few dozen miles from Huntsville. Why, he could have been attacked by one of them himself!

"Don't let her burst your bubble," Fern said, patting her on the back. The graying brunette picked up her tray, as well. "Cherry's not happy unless somebody's world's coming to an end—preferably hers. It's nice to see you all sparkly and flushed over something with two legs, for a change."

She was all that? "Thanks," Frankie murmured, more than a little bemused.

As Fern left, Benny started filling her orders. "Hey, kiddo, guess what? You know that old navy buddy from Minnesota I've been talking about? Well, he's done it. He and his nephew are moving down. He called me just now from the Texas-Arkansas border. They'll be here sometime tomorrow, and he's interested in taking the job as The Two-

Step's cook. This is the guy who makes *the* world's best onion rings. Spread the word—the grill's reopening again!"

Preoccupied with her own adventure, Frankie had all but forgotten about Benny having discussed that. "I will," she assured him. "Congratulations!"

But pleased as she was for her boss, her real pleasure came at closing time when they locked up and she headed for Petunia. Cherry's pronouncement had assured her of one thing: Johnny wasn't an escaped felon. Since Cherry brought up the topic, she would have said if she'd heard anything else. And Cherry was a reliable source for *all* kinds of bulletins.

Granted, this happiness she was feeling could well be temporary... but it didn't keep her from humming all the way home.

Johnny stared at the snake—Stretch, he corrected himself—who lay between him and Frankie on the truck's—*Petunia's*—bench seat, and stared back at him. He scratched around his bandaged wound, wondering if he would ever get used to everything having a name, let alone remembering them. He wondered if all three of them would make it to Houston.

"Are you sure you don't mind coming with me? Is your head giving you problems? I thought the wound looked much better when we put new antiseptic on it this morning."

"It's itching because it's healing, sweetheart," he said, immediately forgetting about his own discomfort to assure Frankie. "I'm fine. Everything's going to be fine."

Ever since Saturday when old man Miller had dropped by to report that the zoo had phoned and wanted Stretch on Tuesday, she had been acting like a mommy bird who knew she had to give up her nestling and was dreading the moment. It had been an experience, but one that had reinforced his respect for her, as well as strengthened the hold she had on his heart.

She cared, really cared about the creatures she took under her wing. Heaven only knew how she'd survived the partings, let alone the losses up until now. He was relieved for her that the weekend was over and that D-day would be over soon, too.

"Does he look stressed to you?" she asked him for what had to be the fifth time in maybe thirty-something miles.

He looked from her to the snake glaring at him while she drove with one hand and stroked it with the other. "No. He looks like he always does, as if he'd like to play necklace with me."

"Johnny. You're sweet to try to cheer me up with jokes."

But he hadn't been joking. That was the problem, and her whole intuition system had been off all weekend. Even work hadn't helped. In fact he thought she was more depressed when she came home. "Are you going to be okay with this?" he asked her, coming to a conclusion within himself. Because if it was a toss-up between her peace of mind and him not liking one of her pets...

"Of course! Probably. Well, I will be eventually." She shot him a wry look. "I do know this is for his own good. It's just that I worry he's going to miss the human contact. He's such an affectionate little guy."

Johnny couldn't begin to agree, but that didn't keep him from thinking she was one special lady. She could find something good to say about anything. He was living proof of that.

It still stunned him that she'd taken him in the way she had. He represented an incredible risk to her, and yet she had made him as welcome in her home as anyone could be. More.

God, but she made him feel things. Just looking at her as she sat there in an oversize T-shirt and jeans tied him in knots. She had a light that began in those huge baby blues and just kept going. When she smiled, which was often, the voltage almost doubled. And that hair... No doubt some stylist somewhere would say there was too much, that it was overpowering for someone as slight as her. True, she had yards and yards of curls in every shade of blond, but he thought it glorious. *She* was glorious.

"Hello?" she singsonged. "Where'd you go?"

"Nowhere, believe me. I'm right here."

"Then tell me, now that you got to see Mr. Miller for a second time, has your opinion of him changed?"

Johnny abandoned the fantasy he'd been weaving of the two of them and frowned at her question. As with the snake, it took no time at all to form a reply. "He's suspicious of me."

"You said that the first time."

"And my opinion stands."

"He's just protective of me."

"True, and I respect him for that, but...he asks too many questions."

Frankie took a moment, clearly wanting to consider that. "I don't think he's been asking many more than when I first arrived on his doorstep to talk to him about settling on his property. You have to remember, he's a widower and his children aren't close enough for frequent visits. He gets lonely. Conversation is his entertainment."

"You heard him, he told me again that I look familiar," Johnny replied, fingering the receding knot at the back of his head.

The old man had eyed him closely from behind thick wire-rimmed glasses, his expression not exactly suspicious, but not what one would call welcoming, either. Of course,

Johnny knew the condition of his face didn't inspire instant trust—Frankie was definitely one of a kind for responding to him the way she had—but there had been something in the farmer's expression....

"Mr. Miller is always mistaking one person for another," Frankie reminded him, as she had the other day. "You should hear him when he's trying to tell you about a movie he's been watching. He'll go on and on about how great the actor or actress was in it, how they were equally good in several other films—which he'll give you a synopsis of from beginning to end—only to stop suddenly and realize he was thinking of the wrong person after all."

But what if this time the nosy coot had been right? he thought. What if his picture *did* show up in some paper or magazine? That could make Frankie vulnerable in ways he could only imagine. "I just don't want to get you into any trouble."

"Did he go home and phone the police the other day? Has anyone knocked on the door since to arrest you? Adopt you? Anything?" Frankie shot him a tender look. "I'm more concerned about those nightmares you keep having."

There was that, too. He had only to close his eyes and the terror began. Last night's dreams had been the most intense yet. Sometimes he'd been that kid again, being dragged kicking and screaming up endless flights of stairs, down pipelinelike halls by some emotionless, indescribably cruel being. And always he would end up in that cramped, dark place struggling not to weep from the pain that had been inflicted; trying to keep a handhold on his sanity by imaging how he would destroy his jailor.

Then as thoughts of revenge, *murder* filled his mind, things would change, and his tormentor became a sultry woman... or had it been two women? The faces changed. But not so his hatred for them.

In the end, there would be a veil of red over his eyes. Blood? Even now in broad daylight the urge to open his mouth and scream was barely repressible. When he'd actually had the dreams he'd woken up all the animals in his torment, and they'd started a caterwauling that should have roused the dead in the next county. Yes, the dreams rattled him to his core.

"There's a message to the child," Frankie continued, not put off by his silence. "I keep thinking that seeing yourself that way is your mind's way to deal with the trauma of what you went through the night I found you."

Johnny disagreed. Oh, he saw nothing wrong with her deduction, but if true, it was damned embarrassing. It would suggest he was someone who ran from his problems . . . that he was unworthy of a brave lady like her. Being worthy of Frankie was of great importance to him. Almost as important as trusting she was safe around him.

"And I think you have enough to deal with right now, without getting all tangled in another discussion about my problem." He reached over to brush aside several strands of hair the wind had whipped in her face, not about to miss any excuse to touch her. "Why don't you let me focus on you for a change?"

He got the opportunity a short time later after Stretch was presented to the experts in the snake house and they were on their way back to the parking area. Johnny spotted tears creeping out of the corners of Frankie's eyes. She tried to hide them, of course; she ducked her head behind her shaggy bangs and the rest of that wonderful, wild mane of hers. But he saw, and her sadness made it impossible to keep his distance. Not that he wanted to.

He wrapped one arm around her shoulders and gave her a gentle squeeze. Then he cupped his free hand before her to signal for the keys.

"You don't have a license." Her usually clear voice had grown thick from repressed emotion and carried a hint of the East Texas drawl, as he was beginning to notice it did when she was her most distressed.

"True." On the other hand, she wouldn't be able to see ten feet ahead of her with all those tears blinding her. "So I'll drive carefully. Come on, hand them over." He hoped he sounded convincing, since it struck him too late that he didn't even know if he *could* drive.

Frankie was convinced. She exhaled in a way that indicated she was relieved to pass over the keys.

They didn't talk again for a while. Petunia required concentration, thanks to a wobbly front end and a dubious brake system. So did the relentless Houston traffic, which gave new meaning to the term "defensive driving."

By the time they were on the north side of town, Frankie had gone through almost a dozen tissues. But the more pine trees they spotted intermingling with the minimalls, sleek office buildings and manicured condominium complexes, the more peaceful she became.

"You know he really is going to like it there," she said at last, with the beginnings of a smile. "Did you see him head straight for the partition that separates him from the larger area? That was the female boa they were going to pair him with on the other side."

"How about that." In truth Johnny hadn't looked. All those snakes had given him the creeps. "So you see? He's already making new friends. Doesn't that make you feel better?"

"Mmm. I'm fine now."

If he'd had any doubts, they were discarded the instant she spotted the puppy.

"Will you look at that?" She nearly did a one-hundred-eighty-degree turn despite her seat belt. "That poor little guy is parked in that car over there with barely a window cracked, and it's nearly high noon! Why, it must be over ninety degrees already. Take the next exit, Johnny. I'm going to make a citizen's arrest."

He slowed, he shot her a few curious, then dubious looks, but he didn't exit. That won him a squeaky cry of indignation from her.

"What are you doing!"

"Maybe the owner only stepped into a store to buy dog food," he said, in an attempt to be the voice of reason.

"Ha! More than likely it's some airhead getting her nails done. Go on, get out at this exit. *Johnny!*"

Amnesia hadn't affected his hearing. The instant her angel-sweet voice took on that edge, he realized that when it came to things she cared about, Frankie could be a little Hun. As he circled back two blocks and turned into the small shopping center, he wondered what he was in for. Then he saw the pup panting in the car and knew he could find a few choice words to say to the owner himself.

He barely had Petunia stopped before Frankie jumped out and began trying all the doors on the sturdy older model sedan. The golden retriever pup began barking, and licking and scratching at the windows.

Johnny cringed inwardly when the door of the beauty salon burst open and someone wearing a sheet of fuchsia plastic with neon-blue goop on her head charged toward them. "Er... Frankie. We have company."

"What do you think you're doing? Get away from there! *Help!* Someone call 9-1-1!"

Frankie rose to her full, though inferior height and matched the hefty woman glare for glare. "That's right, someone call 9-1-1, because this puppy's going to need it after she finishes frying his poor brain!"

Johnny scratched at his wound again. His angel had impressive lungs.

Maybe the woman was put off by that declaration. Maybe she was amazed that someone as compact as Frankie could yell like a water buffalo in the throes of labor. Maybe she saw the steel in her baby blues. Whatever the reason, Johnny was impressed when the older woman took a step back and her expression changed to one of uncertainty.

"The window's cracked." She recovered enough to point with pride, although the gesture was ruined by her shaking finger. "He's getting air."

"Not nearly enough. How would you like to be locked in there wearing a fur coat?"

The question had an interesting effect on the overweight woman. She unrolled the magazine she'd been slapping against a thigh stouter than Johnny's and began using it as a fan. "Well, how should I have known what I was supposed to do? He belongs to a resident at my apartment complex who ran out on me owing two months' rent. I was only going to take it to the pound after I finished here."

"Oh! *Oh!*" Beet red with fury, Frankie dug into her purse, drew out a bill and thrust it at the woman. "Here. At the pound they would have asked you to donate toward his care until he was adopted. *If* he was adopted. Now open up and let me have him."

As soon as the woman did, Frankie ducked inside and scooped the excited puppy into her arms. "Come on, little guy. Everything's going to be all right," she cooed, carrying him to Petunia. She never gave the stunned woman another glance.

"Isn't he gorgeous?" she asked Johnny, as they merged back into freeway traffic. "See how happy he is that we saved him from that terrible woman? Johnny, take the next exit."

What for, this time? Good grief, if she'd spotted another animal—

"I need you to hop inside that convenience store up ahead and get him a bottle of water. Take the money from my purse. Please? This little guy has to be dehydrated, and I don't think he'll make it all the way home without something to drink. Feel his nose. It's so warm and dry."

So this was how it happened. Johnny couldn't help but smile as he made the exit. No wonder the woman had looked as if she'd had a close encounter with a tornado. Frankie had even surprised *him* with her determination and spunk; and he'd thought he'd seen every side of her over the past few days.

He came out of the store with the water, but also a box of puppy food. The small dog already looked happier with the fully opened windows and loving attention. By the time Frankie fed it the water in her cupped palm and a few kernels of the dry cereal, its big brown eyes were sparkling with adoration.

"What should we name him?" she asked, as Johnny once again directed Petunia onto the highway.

We. He did like the sound of that. "Lucky," he replied, thinking that he and the pup had a great deal in common.

"Very funny. The girls at the club suggest that every time I bring someone new home. Can't you tell? This is a special little guy."

"In that case you're going to have to call him Johnny, Jr.," he replied, feeling her fill yet another empty chamber in his heart. "Or how about Maury, Too?"

She groaned. "Okay, I know I say that about everyone I bring home, but that's only because it's true."

"On behalf of your adoptees, I thank you." But as sardonic as he sounded, he felt a unique and sharp pleasure. If only heaven would allow him to continue on like this, to let him stay here. He had nothing—even the clothes on his back were a gift—and yet his life felt ... full. Perfect. He shot Frankie a possessive look, almost relieved that she missed it. "His hair's the same color as yours. How about Blondie or Goldie?"

"Goldie's kind of cute. I like Happy, too. Have you ever seen anyone so eager to be loved?" she added, nuzzling the dog.

Oh, yeah, babe. All I have to do is look in a mirror.

When he noticed the puppy alternately nipping and scratching at Frankie's belt buckle, he laughed. "There you go. Call him Buckle."

"How cute! But how about just plain Buck?"

"It seems like a big name for such a small dog."

"He won't be small for long. Look at the size of these paws. He's going to be every bit as huge as Maury."

"But are you sure he's a *he?*"

With a quick, mischievous grin, Frankie lifted up the pup and held his belly before Johnny's face. "Any more questions?"

"I guess not," he replied, and their laughter was as effusive as the brilliant Texas sunshine.

Frankie never imagined she would enjoy the day so much, and she wished it could have lasted and lasted; but inevitably it was time to leave for the club again. She faced the prospect of a difficult night with dread.

She hadn't told Johnny about the problem that had developed there. She hadn't wanted to burden him with her dilemma, and had let him think she'd been preoccupied by Stretch. He had his own worries to contend with, and while she was glad he seemed to be growing more confident and trusting around her, there were psychological doors he re-

fused to open to her. Maybe to himself, too; she simply
didn't know.

She'd also been hoping that what had happened Monday
at work was an anomaly. She'd prayed that she'd taken care
of things. But soon after she arrived at The Two-Step Tuesday night, she had to face an unpleasant fact: along with
Benny's new cook had come trouble.

Benny's old navy buddy, Stan Mahar, appeared to be a
nice man. Friendly and funny, he seemed eager to make a
new life for himself in Texas. It was also apparent to everyone that he bore a deep affection for Benny. But his nephew
was another matter entirely.

Clever, attractive, but disturbingly sly, Deke Mahar made
it clear from the moment he'd been introduced to the gang
that he planned to carve himself out a piece of territory here.
What Frankie found disconcerting was that his idea of territory included her.

He wasted no time in asking her out.

She didn't hesitate in turning him down.

It wasn't the matter of Deke being an ex-con; if anyone
was known for giving people a second chance, besides
Benny, who knew of the young man's run-in with the law,
it was her. But he lacked a sense of sincerity that she looked
for in any relationship, and a respect for others.

When he failed to be put off by her refusal, she relied on
Johnny's presence in her life. Deke treated the news that she
was involved with someone as inconsequential, and after
only an hour of Tuesday's shift, under the pretense of asking her to help him locate something in the kitchen supply
room for his uncle, he cornered her and stole a kiss.

Upset by his aggressiveness and repelled by the amount of
alcohol she smelled on his breath, she elbowed him sharply
in the ribs and snapped, "Do that again and I'm telling
Benny."

"Stop pretending," he replied, unaffected by her blow. "You know you're flattered by the attention. In this nowhere neck of the woods, you have to be starving for the kind of hands-on care you deserve."

Frankie couldn't believe his audacity. "Didn't you hear what I told you?" she demanded, once again forced to step out of his reach. "I'm already seeing someone!"

He shrugged with a casualness that accented his sinewy build. Frankie thought of him as more of a snake than Stretch.

"I heard. But that can be easily taken care of."

"I can't believe anyone as nice as Stan is related to a jerk like you."

She'd stalked out of there as angry as she'd ever been. Nevertheless, she would have been willing to leave it at that; but he didn't give up. The good news for her was that the other girls caught on that something was amiss.

"He gives me the creeps," Holly declared when she and Frankie crossed paths in the ladies' room during a break. Just back from vacation, the raven haired waitress was no more pleased with Benny's addition to the club than Frankie. "If he calls you to help out again, ignore him. I'll back you up if he makes a fuss."

"Tell Benny!" Fern insisted, when she caught Deke staring at Frankie once too often.

"Deke will only deny it." She'd already noticed his ability to put on an entirely other face when dealing with their boss.

"So what?" Cherry whispered furiously from behind them. "The guy's walking trouble. Benny's wearing blinders because of Stan, but he doesn't need the likes of that one around."

But Frankie asked them not to say anything to their boss because Benny looked happier than they'd seen him in ages.

She didn't want to be the one to tell him that his friend's nephew was a troll.

She thought she would never make it to closing time. Then she found regretting her decision not to report Deke's behavior to Benny.

Only minutes after leaving The Two-Step, she noticed she was being followed.

She instinctively knew who it was. When she'd seen the Mahars' station wagon pull out in her rearview mirror, her heart had nosedived into her stomach with the knowledge that she had more on her hands than she knew what to deal with.

Deke stayed close behind her. At this hour they were virtually alone as they drove down the farm-to-market road. There would be no help from the law, unless she veered up onto the interstate and tried to draw the attention of a state trooper. However, she had her doubts as to whether poor Petunia was up to that.

No, her wisest option was to get home and hope the animals proved as much of a deterrent as they had in the past. This wasn't the first time she'd attracted more attention than she wanted. And now she had Johnny, too—only she shivered at the thought of Johnny getting into a fight. Not her tender, caring Johnny who ever since he'd seen those marks he'd left on her wrist that first night he'd grabbed her, had treated her as if she were made of glass.

Please, God... let Maury be enough.

By the time she pulled into her yard, she was shaking. Maury started barking at the strange vehicle as soon as it followed her over the cattle guard. But to her surprise, Deke didn't hesitate in getting out of the car and heading for her.

Frankie scrambled out of Petunia and backed toward the deck. "Stay away!"

"You know you don't mean that. Just get that mutt to shut up, and we'll have a little party of our own to wind down the evening."

"My dog will bite!"

Deke Mahar wasn't deterred, and despite Maury snarling at her side, he kept coming, grabbed at her.

"Let me *go!*"

She scratched at his face and screamed. Maury leaped against Deke, his mouth aiming for Deke's arm. But the man had excellent reflexes and knocked him back against the deck. Then the screen door burst open and Johnny appeared.

"Get your hands off her!" he commanded.

Six

Maury jerked at the sound of Johnny's lethal warning, and with a low growl, pressed against Frankie's legs. Even Frankie found herself shocked at the depth of coldness in his voice. She'd known he would come to her defense, of course; but she didn't expect the murderous gleam she saw radiating from his eyes.

The shepherd saw it, too, and with a growl, shifted against her legs, unsure whether he had to protect her on one or two fronts. It countered Deke's hold, and began throwing her off-balance. Then Johnny leaped off the deck at Mahar and she had no hope of recovering.

Johnny hit Deke in the shoulder, sending him flying. The force of the blow sent Frankie in a different direction, minus a handful of her T-shirt, and Maury ended somewhere in between. The dog recovered first, scrambling to his feet to immediately sink his teeth into Deke, who'd kicked him as he went down. After that, Frankie couldn't see for several seconds due to Buck, who dashed from behind the deck steps and leaped on her with relief and welcome.

"Oh, God...sweetie, get off," she gasped, trying to concentrate on the punches and curses going on a few yards away. Sweeping the puppy into her arms, she squirmed to a sitting position.

By the time she turned around, Johnny was shoving Deke into his car. "And don't ever try coming back!" he growled at him.

Maury offered his own snarl, and soon dirt and gravel flew everywhere as Deke sped away. Frankie watched her rescuers exchange looks. Johnny murmured something she couldn't hear to the German shepherd before slowly turning toward her.

Who was he? As she stared at him standing there barefoot, wearing only a pair of the jeans she'd bought him, the question came as starkly as it had the first night. She thought she'd begun to form an answer, but the easy yield to violence she'd just witnessed, the sudden remoteness now...

"Are you okay?"

She didn't know if she could respond to this stranger.

"Frankie?"

The iciness vanished. That amazed her. If she hadn't witnessed the scene herself... His cold rage was replaced with the warmth and tenderness she'd come to attribute to *her* Johnny. He hunkered before her, very large and real, the floodlights illuminating the sheen of sweat clinging to his chest hair. With a gentleness belying his size, he touched her hair, her bare shoulder. She started belatedly remembering what had happened to her T-shirt.

"Sweetheart, don't look at me like that. Are you hurt?"

"No. I'm fine...now."

"Who the hell was that?"

It took her two tries to get the words out. Her throat was so dry. "Deke Mahar. The new cook's nephew. They got into town this weekend. Stan's a longtime friend of Benny's. Benny is so happy to see him that he hasn't noticed what a jerk Deke is."

"And has this—harassment been going on since they arrived?"

He wasn't going to like her answer. As she expected, the tenderness in his eyes chilled several degrees. Buck even decided it was intimidating, and he squirmed free to run and visit Maury.

"Hell," Johnny growled. "And here I thought you were only brooding over that damned snake." He lifted her chin. "You're going to fill Benny in first thing in the morning, right?"

"Yes. As much as I don't want to hurt his feelings, I have to. If you hadn't stopped Deke..."

When she shuddered, Johnny shifted onto his knees and drew her into his arms, tucked her head under his chin. "You don't know what I thought when I heard your cry. And then to see him coming at you..."

"It's over now."

But they continued to cling to each other, as if the connection was the only way to convince themselves. The night sounds mellowed to a hum of crickets and tree frogs. Maury, Buck and the others settled back down in their favorite sleeping spots with contented sighs. It was time to let go, to put a little distance between herself and Johnny; to get inside before the mosquitoes took note of the body heat emanating from them in stronger and stronger waves. But just the thought of ending this perfect moment in time had Frankie fighting back a sob.

With a muffled oath, he lifted her into his arms and carried her inside. He set her on the kitchen counter—a strangely appropriate place, she discovered, realizing it put her nearly at eye level with him.

He framed her face with his hands to keep things that way. "Tell me the truth. Are you hurt?"

"Listen to you," she murmured, trying not to want, to need too much. "Save a girl's life and you act as if that gives you the right to turn into an autocrat."

He touched his forehead to hers. "No jokes tonight. No teasing. Tell me what's wrong."

"Nothing...except how you make me feel whenever you touch me."

He grew very still. "I want to kiss you so badly, it hurts. Make sure you mean it if you say it's okay."

"Yes."

She even closed her eyes in anticipation of his lips against hers. Instead, he spread the ripped cotton of her T-shirt and pressed a kiss to the bare skin just above her breast.

His mouth hot against her cooler, taut skin came as a surprise, but a welcome one, as did the masculine roughness of his day-old beard. He made her feel weak and yet strong at the same time, and she combed her fingers into his hair to seek more.

The two fans that provided their only cooling blew her hair over them like a veil. Its caress over Johnny's bare back and shoulders wrung a low groan from him and suddenly he was seeking her mouth in that blind, compulsive way that told her the control he was trying to maintain was slipping fast.

If anything could block out, albeit temporarily, the nightmare that had almost claimed her, the one that continued to haunt him, it was the moving, restless kiss he initiated. It spoke of steamy desire and unsatisfied hunger; and yet he took his first taste of her without the tongue-tangling joining she knew they'd both been wanting. Instead, he denied himself and her, to score a series of ardent kisses down her throat.

It was his hands—his strong, long-fingered hands—that failed at patience. They moved over her from shoulder to knee and back again, streaking fast to her breasts when his mouth descended, kneading then cupping her to receive his nuzzling against her over and over.

She thought it a heavenly torment, until he pushed the T-shirt up, pulled her bra down, and covered her with his mouth. Then Frankie knew that she needed to discard her definitions, because he was teaching her new ones.

She wanted to sink back, back like a falling feather, an offering to madness, or hope—whichever he represented—taking him with her. She pictured them together in the bed that so often she'd felt was too large for one. Together they would fill it, or make a fine mess of the sheets trying. It thrilled her to realize that there was no shyness, no pretense when it came to his body, her body. They were stunningly honest in their responses to each other, and they would be good together. Unforgettable.

Except for one small thing, Jonesy. And don't say you've forgotten that there's probably someone waiting for him in another bed somewhere.

"Oh, God."

The stark, unwelcome thought made her all the more sensitive when he drew her hips to his and held her as close as they could get while still wearing some clothes. When he sought her mouth for the kiss she knew would finish her, she desperately averted her face.

"Frankie."

Her name was a roughly tender entreaty that had her hugging him tightly, even as she knew she had to let him go. "I'm sorry. I'm so sorry."

"Shh...just kiss me, sweetheart."

"Johnny, you know we're going too far. We have to stop."

But the fever that threatened to devour her was doing the very same thing to him. His tortured groan, and his restless, stroking hands issued the more profound message that her words were easier spoken than fulfilled.

He lifted her off the counter and wrapped her legs around his waist, moved her against him. "It's not a crime or sin to feel the way we do about each other," he rasped against her neck. "This is good. It's honest! It's *right.*"

So right she could have died from the pleasure of it. Especially when he captured her mouth with his and finally began the kiss she'd been dreaming of. But if she succumbed, would she be able to face herself in the mirror in the morning?

She didn't realize tears were streaming down her face until Johnny noticed them and went still. Moving slowly, as if in fierce pain, he lowered her to her feet; and yet he was beyond gentle as he straightened her clothes. Only the slight trembling in his hands and the shallowness of his breathing told her what this was costing him.

"Don't cry. Please...don't," he muttered, brushing back her hair and kissing her forehead as if she were a child.

"I'm not. I never cry."

"Baby, I can't bear it."

"It's so stupid...I'm never this weak and silly." With brutal swipes, she brushed the tears from one cheek and then the other, but the flood kept coming.

Johnny turned her toward the bedroom, clearly unable to look at her anymore. "Go lie down. Take the bed. I know you probably won't sleep, but try to rest anyway."

"Johnny..."

"*Go!*"

His sharp voice propelled her forward faster than any- thing else could have. Even so, she only made a few steps before he grabbed her from behind and pulled her back against his rock-hard body. "Don't hate me, Frankie. In the morning if you want me to go, I will. Just don't hate me for not handling this well."

Of course he didn't want to leave, but Johnny had more to worry about besides nearly losing his head with Frankie— bad as that was, considering the experience she'd just been through with that creep who'd followed her home. That had been reason enough to send her to bed and take his misera- ble self outside to punish it with mosquitoes and animals who thought he was their personal scratching post.

But he'd also experienced some strange reactions when he'd fought with Mahar. He'd sensed a fury in himself that was deep and fertile...unlike anything he'd felt, *as far as he could remember.* That chilled him to the bone.

He was capable of raw, physical violence. Of all the dis- coveries he could have made about himself or his past, he could have done fine without that one. He'd liked having Frankie think he was good, and tender, and kind, even though he'd suspected it wasn't all true. He'd enjoyed the animals' friendly acceptance of him—well, except for the damned lizard that continued to watch him from its vari- ous hiding places and occasionally took a swipe at him when Frankie wasn't around. He wanted to fit in here, in Frankie's slightly offbeat, definitely unique, but sane, fair world. He ached for the peace of belonging, the serenity that came in fully loving.

Instead he'd looked into the eyes of a hard-edged, selfish and mean man and recognized shadows of himself. He'd watched Deke Mahar grab Frankie, and the violation of that simple act had released an anger in him that could have paralleled the liquid fire bursting from a volcano. That's why he'd hustled the man into his car as soon as possible. He'd known that if he'd gotten his hands around the guy's throat . . .

And Frankie had seen the truth, recognized the danger. She was too attuned to the fundamental ingredients in nature to have missed it—she was innocent, not naive—and it had scared her. Tonight he'd recognized his ability to hate, and it was vastly different from what she witnessed in her animals when something invaded their territory or threatened her. What had happened between him and Mahar had been more than a male, king-of-the-mountain contest. It had been a mutual acceptance of the ability to act with malice, and enjoy it.

He was not the simple man Frankie had convinced herself he was when she'd invited him into her home. This changed everything. What happened minutes ago had reminded her of why she couldn't make love with him, and it was worse than the uneasiness he'd felt about finding out who he was. Worse than suspecting he'd done something wrong, which had made him reluctant to seek help from the police.

He now understood he could, *would* knowingly do wrong. Harm. The question was, what should he do about it? What would have more leverage in making his decision, his mind or his heart?

Morning was barely more than a hint of gray when he finally returned inside to make some badly needed coffee. While waiting, he went down the hall to check on her and ended up watching her sleep. She, too, had been restless most of the night; he saw that by the way the sheet was tangled around her more than covering her. That gave him an enticing view of bare shoulder and leg, so much of one that his intense stare drove through her exhaustion and she abruptly opened her eyes for a bull's-eye collision with his gaze.

"What now?" she asked, picking up their mood, their conversation as if there hadn't been the three-hour break in between.

"I was about to ask you the same thing."

"Did you get any sleep?"

"No. You didn't get much, either."

"Not until a few minutes ago." She covered a yawn by turning her face into her pillow, then she sat up. "The coffee smells wonderful."

Johnny watched the sleep shirt she'd changed into slip way off her shoulder, exposing the subtle swell of the very flesh he'd touched, tasted last night. He remembered the flash-fire response of his body, felt it again, and in self-defense he turned away, ready to check on the coffee. But first he had to ask the inevitable question that was burning a hole in his brain.

"Do you want me to leave?"

She didn't answer him right away. When he glanced over his shoulder, he saw she was hugging a pillow to her like a teddy bear. It was crazy to be jealous of an inanimate object, but the green-eyed monster had him by the jugular.

"Where would you go?" she asked without emotion.

She shouldn't let it matter to her. All she should care about was that he was a lie. They both knew it now. He more certainly than she, but it was true. Last night, even without the vehicle of sleep, he'd experienced flashes, images to go with the nightmares. Hazy, gray, confusing... like ghosts they'd appeared to him, only to vanish before he could grasp their full meaning. Who were the women who alternatively seduced and betrayed him? Who was the dominant figure that he was beginning to believe was an older man?

He shrugged. "Turn myself into the police. See what happens."

Frankie flung the pillow aside and, debunking the theory of sleep deprivation, sprang from the bed and brushed passed him. "If I have to listen to garbage this early in the morning, I'm going to need a full dose of caffeine."

"It's not garbage, and you know it." He had no choice but to follow her; he was drawn to her like a magnet. He watched her pour for them both. Her agitation matched his own and yet, even annoyed, she made him yearn to hold her, to possess her. "Deke Mahar and I have more in common than you and I do."

With a scathing look she replaced the pot, pushed one mug toward him, and wrapped both hands around hers. "If you're intent on doing this to yourself, go ahead. But I'm not going to help you."

"It's true. You saw it last night, and it frightened you."

"*He* frightened me. What could have happened frightened me."

"And what about us? What if I hadn't stopped last night? What if I ignored what you said and took you the way I wanted to? My God, you'd just been assaulted, nearly raped by a guy, and there I was—"

"But you didn't!"

"This time. What about next time?"

"You won't."

"How do you know!" he roared.

Her hands shook and coffee sloshed over the rim of his mug, burning her. She barely managed to set it down on the counter without dropping the whole thing. Johnny followed suit and spun her toward the sink where he ran cold water over her fingers.

He couldn't tell who was shaking more—him or her. Self-loathing collected like bile in his belly. *Frankie...oh, God...*

"You see," she said quietly, watching the way he protectively held her, soothed her. "You do the slightest thing to me and it unravels you. Whatever you're not telling me about your dreams, you're not a monster."

Ignoring his sopping hands, he wrapped his arms around her and buried his face in her hair. "Frankie, damn it..."

Although she relaxed against him, she didn't abandon her cause. "You only have to look at me and something changes in you. I can see it, even if you don't want to admit it to me or yourself. And it's that look, those emotions I sensed inside you last night, now that I trust. I won't say I liked glimpsing what I did. I won't say it doesn't trouble me, but it's only a *part* of who you are. Regardless of whether you succumbed to it in the past, it doesn't have to own you or your future."

Her faith humbled him. "I wish..."

Without looking she reached up, accurately touching the backs of her fingers to his lips. "So do I. Just as I wish you'd let me help you."

"You are helping me. You're giving me a place to rest and heal until I figure out what I should do."

"That's not what I meant and you know it."

This time he didn't avoid her. "I won't let you do more until *I* know more myself. Not until I'm sure." He barely resisted turning her in his arms and kissing her the way he ached to. As it was, he knew she had to feel him hard and throbbing against her. Settling for a brief hug, he released her. "What are you going to do about Mahar?"

"I'll go see Benny later this morning. Sundays and Wednesdays are my days off, but this shouldn't be delayed. Besides, Benny will be at the club because it's delivery day."

"Will Mahar or his uncle be there?"

"I don't know."

That wasn't reassuring. "Then I'm going with you."

Her expression mirrored surprise and gratitude, but she also shook her head. "That may not be such a good idea."

He knew what she was thinking. "I'm not looking for trouble. But if Deke Mahar's there, I will be, too."

He would not be put off. Frankie tried. She reminded him about the possibility that he could be recognized, she warned how the police might be called in if there was a fight. She even promised to evict him if he did something stupid, like get her fired. But a few hours later, after breakfast and taking care of the animals, he climbed into Petunia's passenger seat and calmly set his safety belt.

"Great," she muttered, securing her own, "just great. You're not only a stubborn mule, you like to play Russian roulette with life, as well."

"I owe you, Frankie. Why can't you simply accept this as a small repayment for all you've done for me?"

"Fine. I will," she retorted, her chin high as she made a sharp U-turn and directed the protesting truck toward the road. "And I won't shed a single tear for you when they put you in handcuffs and drive off with you in a patrol car—for whatever reason."

"I know," he replied with a fleeting caress to her cheek. "You never cry."

So she'd sounded six months beyond juvenile and he'd seen through her; could she help it if this new, more determined air about him worried her? Things would be tough enough once Benny heard what had happened; if she had Johnny to worry about, too...

To her relief, only Stan joined Benny at the club, and her boss's friend looked more concerned than her boss when she walked in with Johnny. That told Frankie quite a bit, and she wasted no time in introducing Johnny and mentioning she needed to talk to Benny alone.

"Does it have anything to do with Deke?" Stan asked, looking extremely stressed, not to mention embarrassed.

"I'm afraid so."

The older man seemed to age ten years as he exhaled and bowed his head. "That's what I thought. I spent the night at Benny's and when I got back to the motel this morning, Deke was only just coming in. I saw his face, the scratches and busted lip, and I asked him about what happened, but he told me to mind my own business."

"What's going on? What are you two talking about?"

Frankie felt terrible for Benny. As she'd suspected, he'd been so caught up in his excitement over reuniting with his old buddy, that he was clearly out in the cold about what had been happening. She hated to ruin things for him.

As though he'd read her mind, Johnny began, "Deke Mahar followed Frankie home last night, sir." He kept his tone polite but firm. "If I hadn't been there waiting for her, I don't know that she would be here today."

The occasional cigar Benny allowed himself fell from his gaping mouth. "Frankie...Lord Almighty...Stan?"

Stan Mahar's stocky body slumped in his chair, his face seemed to cave in on itself. "I'm sorry, Benny. I don't know what to say. As you know, Deke's coming off one run-in with the law, and that's the real reason we left Minnesota despite the terms of his parole. I thought he'd gotten a good scare doing the six months' sentence they'd given him. I thought he would change, but... It would be better if we moved on."

"'We'? Why both of you?" Benny asked, looking devastated. He barely remembered the fallen cigar and, fumbling, crushed it out in the ashtray. "Tell him to go. This has nothing to do with you. He's well over twenty-one."

"He's my sister's only child. My last close relative. If I can't reach him, no one ever will. I'm sorry, Ben," Stan said, rising. "Frankie."

He left then, borrowing Benny's car; his plan was to return to the motel and get Deke. They would drop off the vehicle on their way out of town, he promised his friend.

"Where will you go?" Benny called after him as Stan paused to wave at the front door.

"Houston, I suppose. I almost headed there from the first during a flash of conscience. Deke is... Deke. I was worried about bringing you headaches you didn't need or deserve." He offered a grim smile. "A person should listen to his instincts, eh?"

Benny made no comment to that, but he did stand. Frankie thought his expression heartbreaking and tragic.

"Good luck to you, Stan Mahar," he called at last.

It was difficult for Frankie to watch, because something had altered between the friends. Disappointment had replaced friendship. That necessary bond of trust was broken.

When Stan shut the door behind him, Benny removed his sailor's cap and smoothed a hand over his thinning hair. "Can you believe that? Not in my wildest dreams... I'm sorry, Frankie," he said, his gaze still reflecting his shock.

"For what, Benny? You couldn't know."

His answering look suggested otherwise. "Don't cut me so much slack. I saw that... young thug looking at you. But I thought with Stan around, it wouldn't come to anything."

Sensing Johnny's displeasure at that, Frankie dismissed the apology quickly. "It's done. Let's forget it."

Benny looked relieved for all of seconds. Then he moaned anew. "What about the kitchen? I've had supplies coming in all morning. Now I don't have a cook. The stuff will spoil, I'll lose a fortune!"

"Maybe Estelle could come in and help in the kitchen," Frankie suggested, wanting to help him think of a solution. After all, she still wanted the best for him, and The Two-Step had proved a comfortable and convenient place of employment for her.

"My wife—The War Department—would *love* to poke her nose in here," Benny said, referring to his wife with the nickname he used when he was feeling most agitated. "Only it's not going to happen. You think I'm upset now, you make me spend every day and night under the same roof with her, and you'll see World War III."

She should have known better than to suggest such an idea for two volatile partners like Benny and Estelle. "Then how about the girls and I try taking shifts for a while until you find a replacement?"

"You four have your hands full as it is."

So he'd noticed, after all, that business had held its own without the timber people. "How nice of you to admit that, Benny. Finally."

"Ah." He waved away her gentle teasing. "Let me think." As he scratched at his nape, his gaze fell on Johnny. He narrowed his eyes. "What did you say your name was again?"

Frankie could feel Johnny tense. "Shepherd," he said, his tone cautious. "John Shepherd."

"What happened?" Benny indicated the small bandage Johnny now wore on his temple.

Frankie took hold of his arm before he could speak. "I ran him over with Petunia. Well, nearly. Isn't that romantic? But he wouldn't be in—"

"I don't know that I'm what you're looking for, Mr.—" Johnny interjected.

"Call me Benny, it's easier that way, and the menu's simple enough—burgers, fries, that kind of thing. We keep it short. Makes it simple for everybody. But it's hot work, and you're basically stuck in the back by yourself all night."

"That wouldn't bother me."

Shocked that he was even considering this, Frankie murmured, "Johnny."

"I would need you to start this evening," Benny continued, ignoring her.

Johnny nodded. "That wouldn't be a problem, but something else might. If you need ID, I can't give you any. You know, for tax purposes."

"Why n— Oh. *Oh.*" He looked crestfallen for a few moments and muttered something under his breath about fate and his life. Then he brightened. "You and Frankie are, er, an item, right? I'm not telling any secret here, am I? Why don't I just add what I owe you to her check?"

How could he suggest such a thing! "Benny, that would hardly be—"

"I accept," Johnny announced. "But it will have to be on a temporary basis only," he told Benny, and ignored that she was now gaping at him. "Until you find a replacement. Fair enough?"

"I'll consider it any damn thing you want as long as you show up tonight." Benny pressed a hand to his chest. "Thank you. You're saving my life."

"Now who's going to save yours?" Frankie muttered to Johnny as they walked out of the club moments later.

Seven

Johnny found Frankie's remark amusing, but endearing, too. He had to repress a smile as they climbed back into Petunia. "Now what did you mean by that?"

"Don't play innocent with me. You know darned well the risk you're taking accepting that job."

"A minimal one if Benny's right about the kitchen being in the back and out of the way."

"But it shares the same hallway where the rest rooms are located. What if someone comes out and walks the wrong way and sees you? Recognizes you?"

Johnny shrugged. "Someone could drive into your yard and do the same thing."

"The girls will question you to death."

"That doesn't mean I have to answer them."

That earned him a feminine snort from his ruffled angel. "That's what you think. Holly will be the least trouble, but not because she's not inquisitive, she just doesn't compare to Fern and Cherry. *Cherry*... You think you're bruised now," she moaned, releasing the steering wheel to clasp a hand to her forehead. "There won't be an inch on you that doesn't feel picked at, poked or probed by the time she's through with you."

Her dramatic flair had him yielding to a soft chuckle. "You're telling me she won't be the pushover Mahar was. Are you going to nurse me again after she's done?"

Frankie found none of that funny. "I'm serious, Johnny. You ask me to let you stay with me, virtually hide out, and now this.... Surely you don't think Deke will be back? You got him to show his true colors. He's just a bully who picks on people weaker than himself."

When she paused to catch her breath, Johnny murmured, "It's a way to pay you back."

"Have I asked you for anything?"

No, and he wished she would. Of course, no amount of money would be able to compensate her for all she'd done for him, and she was too decent to let him love her the way he wanted, without knowing if there was anyone waiting for him.

"I need to do this, Francesca."

Not want, but need. She had to understand some decisions had nothing to do with choices.

He saw her tremble, and wondered if it was one of those premonition shivers? In any case, he wished he was driving; he would have pulled over, taken her in his arms whether she'd wanted him to or not, and reassured, soothed her.

He didn't know how much time they had left together, and he didn't want to spend it with silence or tension between them—well, the nonsexual kind anyway. Something was in the air, a change he could no longer pretend wasn't imminent, and he wanted each moment he had left with her to be sweet . . . full of sunshine and laughter. The best. Just in case.

"You don't cook," she said in a small voice.

"You don't know that."

"You *don't* cook. I had to show you how to operate the coffee machine."

"So I'll learn."

"By *tonight*?"

"Benny said the basics. How hard can that be?"

It wasn't too difficult at all. It just took him a whole package of sliced cheese until he remembered that you have to take the cellophane wrapping off each slice *before* you place it on the burger. And that you never flip the burger again once you've added the cheese. Not even the animals wanted some of his first attempts.

He kept at it. By midafternoon he had a fair idea about what he was doing—at the cost of Frankie not having any hamburger meat, cheese or potatoes left in the place, and the kitchen being in shambles.

He and Frankie weren't in much better shape. She'd stayed close to supervise and support him throughout. They were both dripping from working in the steamy kitchen, not to mention from having spent that much time in such cozy confines. They could be Siamese twins, they knew each other's bodies so well, which only compounded the sexual tension pulsating between them, no matter how much they joked and teased.

"You have to be beat," he said, although she looked absolutely radiant to him. "Since you refuse to take your day off and intend on working tonight, don't you want to lie down in the back and take a nap before you shower?"

"Nope, I'm fine. But you go, if you want to."

Not without her . . . and then they wouldn't get any sleep. They probably wouldn't even make it to work tonight.

She noted his look and groaned. "Stop, Johnny, or I swear I'll drag you outside and turn the hose on you to cool you off."

"Want to wrestle me in the shower instead?" he drawled, deciding he was tired of fighting the obvious. "It's not as if it would be the first time."

"Only if we can take Buck. Remember that we came home to find he chased Samson straight through Samson's mud puddle. I have to get him cleaned up before work, too."

He'd forgotten about the smelly little critter. "I'll bathe him," he said, thinking it would be the least he could do after her helping him all afternoon.

"And who's going to clean up this?" she asked, indicating the messy counters and full sink.

He intended to, naturally. But it was a gruesome sight. "The maid?"

"I'll maid you!"

Not only did she pick up the catsup dispenser and aim, to his amazement, she squeezed. He looked down to see a trail of red all over his T-shirt. "Why, you . . ."

With a screech she raced outside, and already familiar with how fast the minx could run, Johnny charged after her.

"My, my, my. There is so much sexual tension between here and the kitchen," Cherry drawled later that evening as she and Frankie met at the bar, "that it's a wonder the condom machines in both bathrooms aren't going haywire kicking out pretty little packets all over the place."

Frankie gave her a sweet smile. "Shut up, Cherry."

They'd been working for over two hours already and except for sneaking glances and an occasional double entendre, the girls had been behaving themselves with and about

Johnny. Frankie knew that was a result of their having heard about Deke Mahar, and had been concerned for her. But this last remark told her that the reprieve was about over.

"Who is he, sweetie?"

"Cherry, you were introduced. Johnny Shepherd."

The taller woman inched nearer. "Then let me ask this—what's he running from?"

That one, Frankie wasn't prepared for. "Running?"

Cherry pretended to brush away a bit of lint off of Frankie's T-shirt. "Honey, remember me? I know an act when I see one, and that man back there, easy as he is on the eyes, and as hot as he is for you, is no teddy bear."

"You're wrong, Cherry. He's wonderful. Really."

"Yeah, doll, and I was born with hair this color. Don't tell me this is about more than lust. Have you gone and fallen in love with him, too?"

Frankie crossed her arms and glared at her. "That's none of your business!"

"Lord love a duck, you have. And you're worried about something. Besides noticing the way he looks at you, I've watched you follow every one of us when we go back there. Not only do you turn greener than Benny's margaritas, you're concerned. About what? Him? What's he done? Tell Mama all about it."

That was Cherry. Too smart to con, and too persistent to ignore. Frankie felt cornered. "Blast it all! Your timing stinks."

"No one's listening. They're all watching that dumb game, Fern's back with your sweetie trying her own method of interrogation, and Holly's washing out her contact lens in the ladies' room. So tell me, what's the problem? Despite my big mouth, I have been known to help occasionally."

True. She had a good heart. But could she be trusted in this case? Frankie had to admit she could use some input from someone. She was getting so confused...so tired of fighting her own feelings.

"It wasn't a fib about running him over. I almost did—the night you said those convicts escaped. I found him on my way home, beaten, naked and suffering from amnesia."

"Poor guy. What did the doctors say when you took him in?"

"I didn't."

"Are you nuts!" Fortunately, Benny was taking care of a customer at the other end of the bar, but Cherry lowered her voice to a whisper again, "You took a complete stranger home? Girl, you're even loonier than I suspected."

"Don't tell me what I already know. Tell me how to help him. He doesn't remember anything. He wouldn't let me take him to a hospital, and he won't go to the police."

"Why not?"

"He's afraid."

"Of what?"

"That he *is* wanted. That he's done something he can't face. He has the most terrible nightmares, which keep him in doubt about himself and his past. He's asked me for time. That's all."

"But you're adding your heart to the list for good measure, is that it?" Cherry whistled softly. "Boy, when you step off a cliff, you really leap."

"He's a nice man," Frankie insisted, urgently. "He may not think so—though I'll admit the way he did go after Deke surprised me—but he's very gentle, very careful with me."

"So you *are* having an affair!"

"No! But that doesn't mean there aren't...feelings."

This time Cherry's eyes glistened with compassion, and she gave Frankie a spontaneous hug. "Oh, baby girl, I'm sorry."

"Never mind the hand-holding, tell me how I can help him find out who he is without stirring up trouble for him. Have you seen a story on TV or in the newspaper about someone missing in our area? Does he look familiar to you?"

"Nope... and I reckon I do hear and see just about everything going on around these parts. He's not from around here though, is he?"

So Cherry had managed to get him to talk more than a few words and had noticed Johnny's lack of accent.

"You know I can be relentless," Cherry replied, at her wry expression. "I'm guessing north, but not the East Coast. Tell you what I'll do... our satellite picks up local news telecasts from all around. I'll pay closer attention. In the meantime be careful. There's always the possibility this is drug related, and if someone was after him, they wouldn't hesitate to get rid of you, too."

Frankie shuddered. "Don't remind me. I did manage to go back to the area where I found him, but there wasn't anything. It's as if he fell from the sky or something."

"Be still, my heart." Cherry pressed a hand to the pink glass one she wore on a velvet cord. "If that's how they make Martians, sign me up for a one-way ticket. It'd beat beer bellies and birdbrained investment schemes any day."

As amusing as the older waitress could be, she didn't forget her promise. Right after the ball game, she flipped one of the TVs to the twenty-four-hour news station despite some grumbles from the patrons, and when the cousin of the sheriff came in, she probed expertly for news of scandals and stories going on in the county. All the responses came back negative.

"What does that mean?" Frankie asked her at their next opportunity to talk.

"Either no one thought he should be in this area in the first place, or no one's missing him yet."

That could create any number of worries, but at least the prospect of his being a notorious escaped convict seemed less and less likely. It made Frankie wonder—as compatible as they were together, could she live with never discovering his true identity? She thought she could; and she believed he might be able to, as well.

If only they could cure him of his nightmares. Then they would have everything to look forward to.

It was an idea she held close to her heart.

The next morning her theory was tested once again with another visit from Mr. Miller.

"Thanks for bringing over the mail, Mr. Miller, and these fresh vegetables. Your garden's outdoing itself this year."

Frankie beamed up at him sitting on the tractor, and patted the shopping bag full of goodies that he'd given her.

"Yeah, it's not bad. This year the cantaloupes are on the small side, though."

"Oh, but they're tasty," Frankie all but yelled, due to his hearing problem.

"Yeah, they are, aren't they? But hot as it's been, the skins on the tomatoes are kinda tough."

"The tomatoes are excellent. The best I remember."

"Yeah, they are. But those cucumbers, now, they may be going to seed."

Frankie grinned at his shameless invitation to compliment him. "Oh, I'll bet you're just exaggerating."

"Yeah." The old man beamed back at her. Then he looked around. "Don't see your friend anywhere."

"He's still sleeping." Though probably not any longer, she added to herself. Between her yelling and the sound of the ancient tractor, no doubt he was watching them through the slits in the blinds. "He started a new job last night, and he's a bit tired."

"Working, is he? That's a good sign." Mr. Miller nodded his approval. "When I first saw him, I thought that soft heart of yours got itself tied up with a worse layabout than Lambchop over there." He tilted his head toward the donkey, lying in a spot of shade, chewing on the apple he'd brought for her.

"He's a good man, Mr. Miller."

"Still reminds me of someone."

Frankie felt a sharp pain in her chest. She had to work at keeping her smile amused. "When have I heard that before?"

"I know, I know. Maybe I'll remember to look in those old papers I mentioned when I get home."

Don't...don't...don't. "Okay, Mr. Miller. You do that."

"See you got two letters in there from the family. Looks like your mom sent you more coupons, too."

"Would you like to sit and have some coffee or iced tea, Mr. Miller?" Frankie asked, knowing he particularly enjoyed hearing the chatty letters her mother wrote, because she sometimes mentioned him. He was a lonely old man whose children didn't correspond much.

"Oh, can't this morning. Got the lady from the newspaper coming by to take a picture of my watermelons. Did I tell you they decided I won the local contest again this year? Biggest watermelon in the county!"

"Yes, you did, Mr. Miller." Beaming, Frankie nodded. He'd told her three times since he'd arrived. "I'll look for that picture and have you autograph it just like last year's."

"It's a deal." He shifted the tractor into gear. "Be good, now."

Frankie waved and watched Maury and Buck chase after him, barking, until she called them back. Then she carried the vegetables inside.

Johnny had just arrived in the kitchen and was reaching for his coffee mug, and trying to tolerate Honey, who was developing a major crush on him. The bird wanted to sit on his shoulder whenever possible, but he never wore a shirt when he came for his first cup of coffee and her nails were sharp.

"Talk about gossipy old men..." he muttered, wincing as he moved the parrot to the chair.

Frankie sympathized at Honey's mournful croak. As always, her heart did a fluttery dance at the sight of him. "You're just jealous because I coddle him," she teased.

"True." His sleep-red eyes could have melted a thermometer as he met her gaze. "Good morning."

"Morning. How do you feel? You still look beat."

"I think someone ran over me while I was sleeping. In a semi." He poured himself a full measure of freshly made coffee.

"Aw...poor baby."

"Want to kiss me and make me better?"

"Someone's feeling very flirtatious this morning."

"It's your fault."

"I'm so sorry. What can I do to rectify the matter?"

"You don't want to know," he murmured over the rim of his mug. He watched her as he took a first sip. "I've contracted this disease and it feels terminal."

Her own mouth felt impossibly dry. "And what's this disease called?"

"Frankie-itis."

"Tragic."

"It sure does hurt like hell."

It was happening again. The pull, the silent messages . . . the yearning. "You're going to spill your coffee," she said softly, when she'd reached the end of her endurance.

"But you would rather kiss me . . . wouldn't you?"

He was so dear. As with his eyes, even the tone of his voice begged her to admit she was going to ache as much as he would by leaving things unfinished between them. Again.

"Yes. And more."

"I'll live on that for as long as I can."

Frankie took a deep breath. "I must have slept more deeply than I thought. Did you have the dream last night?"

"Amazingly, no. What do you suppose changed things, the exhaustion or the sexual frustration?"

"Johnny." His sarcasm only emerged when he spoke of the nightmares.

He rounded the counter. To head for the bathroom and a shower, she knew. But as he passed her, he swooped down and planted a quick, hard kiss on her mouth before she could avoid him.

Frankie was glad when he continued on his way. It saved them. If he'd seen her lick her lips to savor the caress, his essence, they would both have lost what remained of their willpower.

He was playing with explosives. Johnny knew how dangerously he was testing himself, and challenging Frankie; it wasn't sane or fair to either of them. But he was pretty sure it was dreaming of her—of making wild, passionate love to her—that had held back the darkness last night for the first time since they began. If that's what it took—to lose his mind over her—to save it from some indistinguishable demon, so be it.

However, on his second evening at The Two-Step, Johnny knew that spending more rather than less time around Frankie was tantamount to holding a loaded gun to his head. She had only to show up at the counter to place or pick up an order and sweat began pouring down his back.

Tonight she wore a red T-shirt with silver beading and a sweetheart neckline; and her black jeans . . . they made him yearn to wrap her long, shapely legs around his waist. The thought of other men looking at her made him see red, a deeper shade than her sexy top. He endured the boring task of slicing tomatoes for the burgers, by fantasizing about tugging that neckline lower and tasting the sweet flesh he would expose.

It was inevitable that his mind would forget what his hands were doing. Misdirecting the sharp blade, he watched as he cut himself instead of the tomato.

Swearing, he dropped the knife and grabbed his hand.

Frankie happened to be close and ran around the counter to him. "Let me see!"

It was a nasty cut, but one that looked worse than it was. "Thank heavens," Frankie said, exhaling with relief as she quickly reached for the first-aid kit they kept in the kitchen. "Are you lucky."

She put on a large Band-Aid, then directed him to hold his hand up. "And press your other fingers against the wound to stop the bleeding."

"I have to flip those burgers, angel."

"I'll do it."

"You have tables to take care of."

"They're fine for the moment."

As soon as the orders were ready, she rang the counter bell and asked Holly to deliver them to her tables. When Benny noticed, he came back to see what was happening.

"He's fine, Benny," Frankie assured him, urging him back to the front. But after their boss left, she sighed and shook her head at Johnny. "Some people will do anything for attention."

He watched the fluorescent lights shimmer in her hair. "It worked, didn't it?"

She looked over her shoulder at him, which brought their mouths so close they had to share the same breath. She went still, hesitated, but Johnny had no trouble yielding to what he wanted. He captured her lips with his and initiated a sweet, wild kiss that had him edging closer and pressing himself against her bottom.

She moaned. He groaned. Someone hissed.

They looked toward the counter at Cherry, who glared back at them. "Are you two nuts?" she whispered loudly. "Benny will fire you both if he catches you messing around back here."

"Sorry," Johnny whispered to Frankie, once they were alone again.

"It's my fault, too."

"But I'm not really sorry."

She flashed him the neon smile that stunned him every time he was its beneficiary. "Me neither."

However, she did hightail it out of there and conscientiously stayed away as much as she could thereafter. Johnny felt both relieved and annoyed as hell, his body challenging him in a way he doubted it ever had before.

They couldn't go on like this.

"How long do you intend to keep this up?" Cherry asked her in the ladies' room right after closing.

Frankie didn't pretend to misunderstand. "It's complicated, you know that."

"It's going to get downright painful if you two keep poking at the fire instead of putting it out."

Homespun logic. Frankie never tired of it when it came from Cherry. Despite her raging hormones, she smiled. "And just what do you see as a solution?"

Arching a penciled eyebrow, Cherry put a few coins in the condom machine by her elbow, twisted a dial and tucked the cellophane package into the pocket of Frankie's jeans. "Need I say more?"

"Cherry! He could be married! Engaged! Something!"

The older woman shook her head, adamant. "Don't talk legalities to me when a man looks at you the way *he* looks at you. If Johnny has ties elsewhere, they're either dead or dying. You take care of *you*, girlfriend."

The packet burned in her pocket. Maybe Frankie was thinking of it too much as they went back to work to finish cleaning up. Maybe if she hadn't been so preoccupied, she would have gotten the front door locked, as was her responsibility, and the man wouldn't have been able to burst in and level a shotgun at her.

Holly spotted them first. She dropped her tray of beer mugs and screamed.

The next few moments became a madhouse of cries, gasps and curses, the latter from Benny who began to reach under the bar for his own weapon. But the man in the ski mask was quick to notice him, and ordering Frankie not to move, he redirected the shotgun at him.

"Put it *down!*" he yelled. As if to prove he meant it, he quickly shifted the gun back at Frankie's belly.

Frankie stared, transfixed. She had a life, responsibility...dreams. Why was this happening?

"Everybody on the floor," the man snarled. "Except you sweet cheeks," he added to Frankie.

With squeals and gasps, the girls dropped. Benny came from behind the bar and sank to the floor, too. That left Frankie feeling uncomfortably conspicuous and vulnerable before the man.

"What do you want?" she asked him.

"The cash."

There was something about him, his eyes, through the black mask that seemed familiar, but she told herself it was her catapulted imagination. All she hoped was that Johnny had heard this back in the kitchen and would stay put.

"Benny? I think he wants me to empty the register, okay?"

"Give him what he wants," her boss replied, his voice both shaky and terse.

It was terrible. What made people do things like this? The man had to be either desperate or crazy. Did he think he wouldn't be hunted by the police?

"Just be careful with that thing," she said, looking at the shotgun after collecting the money in Benny's cash sack and coming back around the corner. "Here. Take it and go with our blessings."

The man looked around the room at the others and smirked. "Not quite."

Dread took all the heat out of the room and Frankie began trembling. "What do you mean? We gave you what you wanted."

"Not everything. Turn around."

She gulped, but did as he commanded. Her entire body filled with terror when he grabbed her around the waist and started inching backward to the front door. Did he mean to take her with him? She couldn't do that. *Johnny!*

"Please. Let me go."

"No way, sweet cheeks."

Hearing him address her that way once was bad enough; now he'd really made her angry. She began dragging her feet, thinking, no matter what, she wouldn't go willingly.

"Knock it off!" the man snapped, adding a sharp jerk that nearly forced the air out of her lungs. "Walk."

"Don't!" Benny shouted. "Take me. I'll go with you."

"Shut up!" the man yelled back at him.

"Frankie—oh, Frankie, what am I gonna tell Johnny?" Benny asked, instead. "You know he'll be waiting for you at home, and when you don't come... What do I tell him, Frankie?"

What on earth...? Frankie could have thrown the nearest saltshaker at him. He knew perfectly well that Johnny was in the back.

Johnny wasn't. At the same instant it struck her what Benny meant—that Johnny had somehow managed to get out the back door and circle the building. As they backed out the front door, something struck them from behind. The force of the blow was so violent she heard glass break, her own scream, and the gun discharging.

Frankie wasn't too aware of anything else after that. She was vaguely conscious of falling, of more screams and shouts, the groan in her ear and an impossible weight crushing her. It could have been seconds or hours later when the weight was lifted and she was able to suck sweet night air into her lungs again.

"Frankie! Baby? Oh, God..."

She knew that voice. Dazed, and sore, she was plucked from a bed of glass by a pair of strong hands, and lifted close to an equally strong, wonderful body.

"Johnny."

"Yeah, sweet. Yeah. It's over."

He felt so good. So good. She laughed and wept with relief and hugged him, knowing she never wanted to let go.

But then Benny rushed to them, and once they realized it was over, the girls did, too. Everyone talked at once, and there was more hugging and a few tears. Frankie grew dizzy from being passed from one person to another; at first she thought she'd imagined the sound of sirens.

"I called 9-1-1 before I slipped out back," Johnny told an equally surprised Benny.

He was a hero. Everyone told him, except Frankie. She could only stare as units from the sheriff's department and state police arrived. Instinctively her thoughts turned toward concern for and protection of Johnny.

For his part, he seemed only concerned with discovering the masked man's identity. Johnny tugged off his cap as he lay unconscious on the ground and Frankie saw a grim but satisfied smile cross his face.

"You knew," Frankie whispered.

"Aw...no," Benny moaned, as they all stared at Deke Mahar.

Deke slowly regained consciousness. He recognized Johnny and made a rude comment. The police had to grab Johnny to keep him from diving into Deke.

"Hang on, son," the sheriff told Johnny, placing a fatherly hand on his shoulder. "Let's get a little information from you for our reports, and then I'd suggest you take your lady home."

Information... Frankie met Johnny's impassive look. She went to him and wrapped her arms around his waist. "Can't we go now? I'm not feeling very well."

Johnny's hold on her tightened. "She's had a tough time tonight, sir."

The sheriff looked sympathetic, but explained there were formalities. "It won't take long," he assured them.

It took several minutes, and once he ascertained that Johnny didn't have a Texas accent, he asked a number of other questions that either the night's adventure, or a lack of preparation had Johnny avoiding or only partially answering.

"This isn't much of a welcome to our state," the sheriff said, finally clicking off his pen. "But I'm glad it turned out as well as it did. So," he added, reviewing his notes. "You don't have a phone, but I can locate both of you here or at the Miller place if I have any more questions. We'll be in touch."

It sounded so much like a promise, Frankie's legs buckled. Johnny caught her. "Benny," he muttered over his shoulder, "Frankie's had it. I have to get her out of here."

With that, he lifted her into his arms and carried her to Petunia. As he put her in on the passenger side, the girls called goodbyes.

"You don't have a license," Frankie whispered to him when he got in on the driver's side. "You said as much to the sheriff."

"Let's hope he's too preoccupied to notice or remember."

If he did, the law official chose not to do anything about it, and Johnny soon had the old truck out of view of the club. As soon as he did, he released his seat belt and Frankie's. "Come here," he said gruffly, drawing her across the bench seat and up against him.

Frankie went eagerly, wishing she could climb onto his lap, because even this wasn't close enough. "I was so scared."

"Me, too."

"You were wonderful."

"I was scared to death. When I realized what had happened and saw he had you—" Johnny pressed a kiss to her temple that said the rest.

In reply, Frankie slipped her hand into the V of his ripped shirt, needing the feel of his strong body, the steady beat of his heart, his heat. She yearned to press her lips there, too.

"Do you think the sheriff will want to talk to us again?" she asked him, her cheek against his chest.

"Try not to think about it."

"What if they want you to testify in court?"

"I don't know. I'll leave, I guess."

"Johnny!"

The arm around her became a steel band. "Do you think I want to? But if you think that little chat with the sheriff a few minutes ago was torture, what do you think being on a witness stand would be like?"

All she could think was that if he left, she wouldn't be able to bear it. Something would die in her. The mere thought upset her so much, she couldn't trust her voice the rest of the drive home.

Johnny remained silent, too. At the trailer, they tried to respond to the animals' eager welcome, but neither of them was up to lingering. They didn't even look at each other as they went inside. The emotions churning between them were too strong. Not even wanting to deal with Honey, Frankie covered the disgruntled bird's cage right away, passed Dr. J. in his bed and told him to go back to sleep.

And then she just stood there. Stuck in limbo, afraid of the future, and completely in the dark regarding the past.

Somehow she made herself step to the sofa...shift the cushions that would become her pillow. Then she felt Johnny take hold of her, spin her around.

He was a dark silhouette against the outside security lights. "No more," he rasped, bending to her.

Eight

It was the torment in his voice that decided her. It matched her own, and with a strangled cry, she met him halfway, rising on tiptoe and wrapping her arms around his neck.

Despite the dim light, his mouth found hers with precision. A buzzing began in her ears that had nothing to do with the shotgun blast she'd been too close to, or the fans moving hot, humid air now. It was the walls of their foundering reserve finally crumbling...the echo of good intentions' last breath.

They kissed, and the feel of him wet and strong and hungry, so hungry, triggered the most profound reaction in her senses. She trembled, she soared, she ached in those first frantic moments. He felt the same; she knew by the shudder that racked his body, by the deep moan that rose from him.

Stronger than ever, intent, he carried her to the bedroom and lowered the two of them to her bed. He buried his hands in her hair, and gazed deep into her eyes. His were mostly shadow in the twilight, and yet she felt the tenderness emanating from them as completely as she did his body's power.

"Frankie . . . be sure."

"I am."

"When I think what could have happened tonight . . . Be very sure."

She knew what he meant. They'd kissed before, had come close to yielding to the emotions that drew them like a relentless tide. His words, his look, the tension in him said he couldn't endure that again, especially after what they'd both been through this night. She didn't know how else to convince him that he wouldn't have to, except by taking one of his hands and bringing it to her breast, and repeating, "I am."

He looked down as he covered, then molded her, explored the already beading peak that defied cotton and lace to hide its sensitivity to him. He brushed his thumb over her again and again, until he watched the pleasure in her face grow as sharp as pain.

He knew exactly when to kiss her—just before she asked. It should have been a promise of their beginning. Instead it was more, and less: a vow to be gentle, to give as he took. But the one thing she knew he couldn't give her was the luxury of time. It lent an aura of fragility to their kiss, the moment; and it underscored an intuition that when this night was over, something wrenching and permanent would happen. He kissed her as if this was their end, and intent on absorbing the very essence of her into his being, he would imprint himself on her more permanently than a tattoo for the empty stretch that was their future.

Too much for a first kiss. Yet Frankie clung to him eagerly and offered one thing more—her sensuality. That had Johnny murmuring something dark, something very *un-*

Johnny. But then he'd already been painfully aroused before he'd even touched her.

He rolled onto his back and brought her over him so that he could tug her T-shirt up over her head. Her bra was next, and then together they shredded what was left of his shirt, torn during his brief fight with Deke. When both of them were naked from the waist up, he drew her against his feverish, damp chest, and rubbed her over and over him.

Just when Frankie began to believe it was actually possible to spontaneously combust, he lifted her higher and took her sensitized flesh into his mouth, and showed her a new plateau of ecstasy. His tongue was skillful and relentless, and she couldn't hold back the breathless gasps and trembly sighs as he repeated a pattern of caresses from the pulse point at the base of her throat to her navel.

Dazed, already breathless, she gasped when Johnny rolled her back beneath him, cupped her hips and moved against her, it wasn't enough.

Their hands worked in impressive unison to rid themselves of the rest of her clothes and his. Frankie barely remembered the packet in her jeans in time, and grabbed them, muttering with frustration as she dug out what she wanted.

"An odd but timely gift from Cherry. She said she was tired of us staring at each other."

Johnny kissed her and in a thick whisper said, "Put it on me."

She didn't hesitate.

He was so beautiful and strong, so pulsating with life and heat. She also loved how much power she had over him, how her lightest touch could steal his breath and almost cause him to lose control.

In the end, however, he was the one with the power, and having clearly prolonged the waiting as long as he could, he pressed her back onto the bed and slowly, surely eased into her—deep, deeper, as far as she could take him. Even though she was ready, it was almost too much. She couldn't breathe, couldn't speak, couldn't think. Her entire universe expanded and contracted on the very beat of his pulse.

"Frankie...sweet heaven."

He moved like the ocean, and looked like a pagan rising high above her, only to dive again and again into the slick depths of her body. When she peaked, he swallowed her cry; then he drew her legs high around his waist and followed her over the summit.

Johnny could feel the tiny river he was creating between Frankie's breasts from the moisture dripping off his body, but she felt too good for him to reach for the remains of his shirt and dry them off. Still inside her, he was too selfish to leave her hot, tight embrace.

He wanted her again. Already. It filled him with as much awe as it did joy.

"I knew it would be like this," he said against her throat. When she failed to respond, he lifted himself on his elbows and studied her in the light filtering in through the windows.

His angel. His love. He had no memories of other women to compare her with, but that suited him just fine. Even the women in the dream wouldn't come to mind now; and he wanted no one but Frankie, *Francesca Rose,* in every corner of his conscious and unconscious mind, just as he possessed her body.

Let history begin here. My life. Our life.

He didn't know how to pray. Had he ever? Another question... Would there ever be an end to them?

If he could be granted one prayer, it would be—*Let me have her. Let me have a life with her.*

"Are you all right?" she asked, her fingers a whisper across his back.

He smiled. In typical Frankie fashion, she was thinking of him instead of herself. "Yes." He brushed her damp hair away from her face and kissed her eyebrows, the tip of her nose, as much to apologize for his delinquency as to indulge himself.

"Stay with me."

"I will." How could she think he was through yet? His hunger for her was much deeper than could be sated by this one wonderful but brief joining. Whether or not he recalled his past, he knew that Frankie was who he'd been searching for all his life. And from today on, he intended to tell her, show her, prove it to her. Maybe then he would begin feeling worthy of her. If they were granted the time.

"Tell me," he murmured, running his thumbs along her cheekbones.

"What?"

"More about you." They'd already talked a good deal when he would join her outside when she worked with the animals. But they'd only touched the surface of who she was. "Tell me everything. From the beginning. I have no history. Give me yours. Give us something, someplace to sink our roots. Tell me about your first memory. Tell me about your first crush... traveling with your grandfather... your biggest fear. Write your dreams on my empty slate. Do it, Frankie—I'm so alone. I don't know anything else in the grayness I live in, except that I'm alone."

She was generous. She wrapped her small, surprisingly strong arms around him and hugged him with a warrior's fierceness. She *was* a warrior in a way, one who took care of half-blind dogs, crippled cats, clubfooted donkeys and lizards who hid up on bookshelves and behind herb pots.

"Mud and lace."

It wasn't exactly what he expected to hear. But it was vintage Frankie. On a hunch he asked, "First memory?"

"Yup. I was three and a half, maybe four. Blake and Jason—they're the twins—were playing football and I wanted to be smack in the middle of them. They didn't see me sneak outside to join them. It must have been Easter or Thanksgiving... I know I had on a frilly dress that was impossibly itchy. I landed in the iris bed. Carson got me out and read me the riot act."

"He's the eldest?"

"Mmm. The Dictator. The older I got, the worse he got. I told him once that he could suffocate a slab of granite."

"Ouch. Sounds to me as if his only crime was loving you too much."

"Love, I can handle. He's entirely too focused and intense. I pity the woman he finally marries. If he ever marries."

Johnny wasn't at all surprised that she'd gone toe-to-toe with her eldest brother. Technicalities like family hierarchy meant little to her. It was the principle that earned her respect. "What else? Come on. Tell me things that flash in your head as you look back on your life."

"Oh, I love playing Twenty Questions and 'association.' Okay, let's see.... Spanish moss...palm trees in February...a cow giving birth to her calf under a highway billboard...taking my driving test in the snow...the time my mother slapped me for having an opinion of my own. Is that the kind of thing you meant?"

"Yes. But that last memory was sad."

"Or you can look at it as a growing experience."

"A healthy perspective. And that works?"

"Don't I look healthy to you?"

There was that teasing note in her voice, and the matching twinkle in her eye. Feeling himself stir inside her, he purposely took his time to look down her sleek length to where their bodies joined. "You certainly do."

Her smile grew wistful and she drew his head down toward her again. "I have a confession to make. I want you again."

As she moved her hips against his, Johnny repeated the move and brushed his mouth against hers. "You have me."

Then it began all over—the stunning surge of hunger that came as she triggered the floodgates of his senses. Johnny closed his mouth fully over Frankie's, knowing she was ready and as eager as he was. The beautiful honesty they shared was best evidenced by this—their absolute intimacy.

"I love feeling you grow strong inside me," she whispered, when he broke the kiss to reexplore the delicate shell of her ear.

And her approval made him grow stronger. "Frankie," he breathed, swelling inside her. "Come here, angel." He rolled onto his back and sat her astride his hips. "Soar for me . . . and take me with you."

He didn't close his eyes. Not once. Transfixed, he watched her explore his body, discover the places where her touch excited him the most. He witnessed her sleek form finding a lazy, seductive rhythm that made the sweat break out on his forehead and upper lip. He stared, enthralled at her transformation into a wanton, accelerating the tempo, which propelled her to a place where she had to gasp to get enough breath. Even when she collapsed on top of him, damp and exhausted, and he throbbed from finding his own release, he observed her as she sought a comfortable position on him and succumbed to sleep.

Mine. He stroked her hair. *Mine . . . mine . . . mine.*

He closed his eyes and let sleep take him, too.

* * *

It was later than usual when they woke, but that was because sometime near dawn he'd been roused by Frankie's delectable mouth covering his body with a series of relentless, evocative kisses. *That* had led to an erotic experience that had resulted in his deepest sleep to date.

When he did waken, he immediately tried to stop Frankie, who was faster to wake up than he was, and was sitting up. "Don't leave yet," he murmured, trailing his fingers down the length of her spine.

"Mmm..." She sent him a sweet smile over her shoulder. "I don't want to budge, but the animals aren't going to be patient forever."

"How do you feel?" he asked, concerned that maybe some residual stress from Deke Mahar's attack would linger.

"Wonderful."

"Regrets?"

She sobered somewhat, but her gaze reflected serenity, not turmoil. "No. No, I'm fine... about everything. You?"

"Fine, except that I can't get you to get back in this bed and sleep with me until noon."

Sleep wouldn't be all he had in mind. As she laughed softly and headed for the bathroom, Johnny took in her sylphlike form and felt the inevitable changes in his body. Groaning, he rolled over onto his stomach and buried his face in her pillow.

He let her have a few minutes in the bathroom, and only rose himself when he heard her heading to make coffee. A brief cool shower helped restrain his wolfish thoughts—until he finally headed for the kitchen himself and saw her bending over to set the small dinette table.

The sight of her in shorts and a cutoff T-shirt that barely covered her breasts was more than any man should have been asked to ignore. Silently nudging the inside door half shut on the faces pressed to the screen—and grateful Honey's cage was still covered, keeping the mouthy parrot semiquiet—he came up behind her, took hold of her hips, and brought his flush against her sexy bottom. The lizard was out of sight. They'd come to an understanding and it knew to avoid him before he'd had his first cup of coffee.

"Johnny! You scared me half to— Mmm..."

He shifted one hand to stroke her thigh, and slipped the other under the T-shirt. "I love your breasts," he murmured, nibbling on the side of her neck. "I wish you'd walk around here topless."

"I think I'd... give Mr. Miller a stroke." Straightening, she reached behind her to bring him closer yet.

"Inside. Go topless inside. Or at least don't wear a bra when it's just the two of us here. Please?" He rolled her nipple between his fingers, winning a gasp from her. "Promise."

Frankie dropped her head back against his chest. "Johnny... breakfast."

"Promise."

"I do! I—promise." She barely got that out because he was stroking the zipper panel of her shorts.

"Are you wearing panties?"

"Uh-huh."

"Let me see," he replied, slipping his fingers under the hem. He slipped his fingers into the silky curls and the silkier place beyond. "Oh, damn... you're wet."

When he released the snap on her jeans, she gasped. "Johnny—we can't!"

"Yeah, we can, sweetheart." They had to or he'd explode. Lose his mind. Die.

He tried to find gentleness in his haste to push down her shorts and release himself from his jeans. But whatever finesse he'd possessed, he lost, stunned by this—how she could have this effect on him after all they'd shared through the night. In a way, he was as much her prisoner as he made her with their positioning.

As he coaxed her over the table, he had just enough restraint left to reach into his slipping pants for another of the packets that *he'd* bought last night. His smile was hungry as he remembered the teasing and foreplay that had gone on last night when he'd made his own confession and shown her his stash. He opened the package, slipped it on, and wrapped himself around her.

"Next time I'm going to spread butter all over you," he rasped, easing into her. "Then I'm going to...lick it all off."

With a high-pitched moan, Frankie stretched her arms to grip the sides of the table, and alternately splayed and flexed her fingers.

"Am I hurting you?" he asked.

"No...so good."

For him, too. But not just because it was bold, erotic sex. It was because she trusted him, as much as she desired him. Pressing an openmouthed kiss to the side of her neck, he slipped his hand to the heart of her. She cried out, tensing beneath him.

"Relax. Shh. It's about to get better. So...better." Because she was incredibly soft and welcoming, melting at his every touch, responding to his slightest caress.

His thrusts were deep but fast. Passion demanded he race her. But he followed her eagerly into the throes of ecstasy, and he held her tight as his growing love for her lit a clearer and clearer path for him.

"I don't think I'll be able to repeat that for a day or so," Frankie said a few minutes later. She'd been about to set the skillet on the stove, and the sudden move getting it from the cabinet brought on a tiny spasm.

Johnny immediately came behind her for a gentle hug and kiss. "Damn... too much of a good thing, huh?"

"You could say that again. But I liked it," she added, stretching to kiss his freshly-shaved chin. "Why don't you fill our mugs and I'll start—"

The sound of a vehicle approaching was followed by Maury's sharp barking, then Buck's softer yaps. Frankie and Johnny turned to peer out the kitchen window and saw a familiar four-wheel-drive vehicle pulling in. It was white with overhead lights and the sheriff's seal on the door. Frankie's serene smile froze as she noted there were two people inside it. Sheriff Mills and... a woman?

"Johnny."

She told herself not to panic, but dread filled her anyway. She remembered the anxiety she'd felt last night, the joy, all the emotions that seemed to make the night surreal, the loving too good to be true. It had been a sign. She'd experienced similar moments of precognition just before her grandfather died, and when Pierce had been in that terrible train wreck last year. That didn't, of course, keep her from praying she was wrong.

"Maybe he's just stopping by to check on you," Johnny said, gripping her upper arms and stroking her with his thumbs.

"I hope you're right. But then who's she?"

"There's only one way to find out."

They exited from the trailer, and Frankie called to Maury and Buck. As the dogs retreated to join her and Johnny, Sheriff Mills and the woman slowly emerged from the vehicle.

Johnny sucked in a sharp breath.

"What is it?" Frankie asked him, only to follow his gaze. He was staring at the woman.

Never before had she known such an instant embarrassment at her casual appearance. It was because the woman was the epitome of elegance and sophistication.

Tall and model-thin, she was dressed all in pink—her suit expensive, her jewelry even finer, and her pale blond hair, short and chic. She was glowing in a buffed, manicured and massaged sort of way. Frankie doubted she could compete with someone like that if she spent a year at a spa.

"Mr. Shepherd, Miss Jones." Sheriff Mills tipped his hat and eyed them soberly. "Sorry for not calling first, but you not having a phone and all kinda made that impossible. You feeling all right this morning, Miss Jones?"

"Y-yes, Sheriff. Thank you."

The grandfatherly-looking man nodded and looked back to his companion and then to Johnny, then the ground between his dusty boots. The brim of his straw hat covered everything of his face except his white mustache. "Darn if this isn't the strangest, most uncomfortable situation I've ever found myself in, so you'll excuse me if I pass on some of the small talk and get straight to the point."

"That might be a good idea," Frankie said, frowning at the woman beside him. It hardly surprised her to be ignored in return.

"Mmm. Well, after I got back to my office this morning, I realized why Mr. Shepherd here stuck in my mind so, and why I thought it odd he was so stingy when I asked him for some background information. It's because I believe you aren't John Shepherd at all," the lawman said to Johnny directly. "It's my hunch that you don't have any memory. Are you suffering from amnesia, son?"

"Yes." Johnny spoke the word as if it had to be pulled out of him. He, too, stared at the woman with a combination of confusion and wariness.

Frankie noted that, and how the woman was beginning to smile at him. Softly. Invitingly. Her stomach rolled as if she were on a dinghy in a typhoon.

"Do you recognize this lady?" Sheriff Mills asked Johnny, indicating his companion with his thumb.

"N-no. I mean..." He winced and touched his bandaged forehead.

It was all Frankie could do not to put her arms around him. She knew he was feeling some pain, but she also wanted to ask him what he was thinking, feeling. Most of all, though, she wanted to pull him into the trailer and slam the door. This wasn't right. It wasn't fair!

"I've seen you," Johnny murmured to the woman. "In my dreams."

Frankie clapped a hand to her mouth to keep from crying out. A pain, dull and lethal, tore through her chest. How could he say that? Why hadn't he told her *that* part? Specifics. That the woman had been beautiful...?

"Johnny—"

Sheriff Mills signaled her to be still. "I've had Mrs. Sullivan fly down from Chicago. She was very grateful when she got my call. Mrs. Sullivan? Would you like to see if you can reach him?"

The woman took another step closer to Johnny. "R.J.?" she said, her smile tremulous. She touched his chest with her left hand, the gold-and-diamond set of wedding rings on her finger bright in the morning sunshine. She winced as she noted his old bruises, and the newer scratches from last night's scuffle. "R.J., it's Greta, darling. Don't you remember me?"

He looked positively ill, and it was all Frankie could do not to force her way between him and the woman, and to soothe him because of the panic and, yes, fear she saw in his eyes.

"I only... I'm sorry, I'm not sure. Wh-who am I?"

"Ranier John Sullivan. But don't worry, R.J., I'm here now, and once we get you away from this...and home again, I know your memory will come back quickly. In any case I have Sidney Birnbaum calling in the best experts to help you. You remember Sid, don't you, dear? He's your closest friend. Oh, R.J., I've been sick with worry about you."

The woman leaned forward and kissed Johnny on the lips. Frankie had to curl her fingers into her palms to keep from shoving her into Samson's mud pen. Then the woman focused on Sheriff Mills. Except for a brief venomous glance, not once since her arrival had she deigned to look at *her*. Frankie felt as insignificant as the animals' water trough.

"You've fulfilled my wildest dreams, Sheriff, and saved my sanity. I'll never be able to thank you enough. But may I take advantage of your kindness and ask for one more bit of assistance? I'm terribly concerned the news that R.J.'s been found has leaked to the press by now. Would it be asking too much to provide us with an escort back to our private jet at the airport?"

"Absolutely not," the white-haired man replied, straightening to his own considerable height. "In fact, I was about to offer my personal assistance."

"You're wonderful." She turned her attention back to Johnny and slipped her arm through his. "Then shall we, darling?"

"But I—" Johnny shot Frankie a desperate look.

She knew he was asking her to help him. To tell him what he should do. She would rather he had struck her. Turned his back and walked away. Anything but this! Not after he'd admitted what he had about his dreams! Not considering who the woman was! Didn't he realize he'd already taken away her right to say anything?

She had to try twice to get the words out. "You...you have to go." *Don't make this more difficult for me than it already is,* she telegraphed with her eyes.

"Frankie," he whispered in anguish. "How can I?"

"Go," she mouthed.

"R.J.," came the soft but rebuking voice behind them.

He took one step...two, walking slowly, as if on wooden legs. Greta Sullivan guided him to the vehicle with a show of concern and patience that would have made Florence Nightingale proud—except that in her spike heels, the blonde used Johnny's strong frame for support more than she offered him any. At least that's how Frankie saw the situation, and it broke her heart. Johnny—if he had to be married—deserved so much better.

The sheriff opened the back passenger door for them. Just as Greta was about to get inside, Johnny bolted. He raced back to Frankie.

"R.J.!" Greta cried sharply.

He almost braked too late, almost toppled Frankie over. He threw her off-balance again as he swept her into his arms and crushed her against him.

"I don't know how, but I'll be back," he whispered urgently.

"No, Johnny. You can't."

"Yes!"

"It's *over,*" she cried softly, a little wildly. "Don't you understand? She's your *wife!*"

"But I lov—"

Horrified that he would get the words out, Frankie pressed her fingers to his mouth. "Don't say it. You have to forget that. Forget about me!"

His eyes turned dark, flinty. The skin across his cheekbones looked as if it might tear it grew so tight. She'd never seen him this upset. Angry. A hint of the stranger she'd once glimpsed after Deke Mahar attacked her?

"Are you going to be able to forget me?"

Not until the day she died. But she couldn't let him know that. She had to make it possible for him to go back to his real life. He might not understand now, but someday he might—and forgive her.

"Frankie, for the love of heaven—"

"Goodbye . . . R.J." She eased out of his arms, stepped away from him, although she had no idea how she stayed on her feet. Everything about her was spinning, spinning out of control.

He stared at her as if she'd lost her mind, or had turned into a stranger he no longer knew. In that case she thought they were even. She didn't know who Ranier John Sullivan was, either.

Without another word, he returned to the sheriff's truck.

Frankie made herself watch as Sheriff Mills made a U-turn; watch until they were passing over the cattle guards. Until they disappeared down the farm-to-market road.

Buck moseyed over to where the truck had been, sniffed and whimpered. Maury lay down next to Petunia as if to wait for Johnny's return.

Frankie couldn't bear it a moment longer. She ran inside, barely making it to the bathroom before she became violently ill.

Nine

Ranier John Sullivan. R.J.

As the small jet rose over the green East Texas landscape and executed a neat turn north, Johnny knew the name was beginning to mean something to him. But it was giving him one hell of a headache on top of the heartache he was already suffering since Frankie's rejection.

He looked out the small window on his right and searched among the increasingly tinier buildings dotting the lush landscape for something that would look familiar. If only he could see the Silver Duck one more time. Frankie hadn't meant what she said. She couldn't. She'd just been thrown off-balance, as he'd been.

"She's your wife!"

The pain worsened as he remembered her words. Grimacing, he glanced at the woman sitting in the seat across from his. His wife. Greta. Could he have fallen in love with someone like this artificial creature before him?

She was attractive, of course, in a refined way. But he sensed a purposefulness to everything she did, a sharpness that made her cool elegance remote. Hard. Since they'd parted company with Sheriff Mills and boarded the unmarked jet, she'd been giving clipped orders to the three-person crew. This was definitely a woman in control. Had she controlled "R.J.," too? Somehow he found the idea unacceptable.

As the flight attendant brought the champagne she'd ordered, she took the long-stemmed glass and settled back in her seat with a satisfied smile. "Have some, R.J. It's your favorite brand."

"No, thank you," he said politely to the young man holding the tray with the second glass. As the man withdrew, he watched Greta shrug and sip. It seemed a little early to him for alcohol.

"You really gave us quite a scare, R.J. And that little number back there in Hicksville." She shook her head. "Now that was really beneath you, though I suppose you couldn't help yourself, given your obvious condition."

"Frankie saved my life."

"In more ways that one, hmm?" Greta's green eyes turned frosty. "Well, I'll tell Sid to order you the appropriate tests. Although it's the least of my worries, the little slut looked as if she's traveled a few miles in that trailer. We don't want you transmitting anything communicable, do we, darling?"

As she raised the glass toward her lips again, Johnny lunged forward and knocked the glass out of her hand, sending it flying across the plane and shattering against the far window. Despite the piercing pain in his head, he fixed his narrow gaze on the shocked, fearful woman.

"My God . . . Greta!" Maybe it was the pain of losing Frankie, or maybe it was due to enduring Greta again, but somehow his memory was coming back to him with brutal clarity. "What have you done?"

"I was only—"

"Not another word." He pointed a shaking finger at her. He felt such rage at her duplicity and deceit, he could barely speak. "Not one damned word."

Frankie ignored the dogs barking and the knocking at the door and hugged the pillow that Johnny had slept on. She exhaled shakily and wondered if she was going to die from the pain.

It had been the worst experience of her life, having to watch him get into the truck with his wife several days ago. She'd felt as if her life's blood had been draining out of her. She didn't remember how she'd gotten through the day, or driven to The Two-Step later that night. She'd barely managed to tell Benny that he no longer had a cook—that Johnny who wasn't Johnny at all was gone—before she'd collapsed.

Summer flu, she'd insisted once she'd come to on the couch in Benny's office. Benny, dear soul, hadn't believed her for one second and had closed the club himself and brought her home. Holly had spent the night. Ever since, either she, Fern or Cherry had been stopping by on a daily basis to check on her.

"Frankie." Cherry used the key she and the girls had had and let herself in. "Damn it all, you're starting to get on my nerves."

The older woman's slip-on sandals flapped noisily as she made her way down the hallway to the bedroom. One glance at Frankie and she grimaced. "You look a sight."

"Go away, and then you won't have to look."

"You'd like that, wouldn't you. Then you could just rot here, play martyr." Cherry tossed her huge straw purse on the bed and took hold of Frankie's wrist. "Well, it's not going to happen, sweet pea. Today you're going to rejoin the land of the living."

Despite Frankie's protest, she dragged her off the bed and into the bathroom, where she turned on the cold-water faucet in the shower, then shoved her inside. Frankie screamed.

"That's right," Cherry drawled. "Use those lungs to do more than whimper and whine about what a rotten deal you've had."

She hadn't whined. She hadn't even shed one tear! "Cherry—I'll kill you!"

"Tell me about it after your hair's washed," Cherry snapped back, just before she walked out of the bathroom.

Frankie furiously adjusted the water taps and stripped off the sleeper T-shirt that was beginning to weigh a ton. God save her from meddling people, she fumed, her teeth chattering as cold water pelted her naked body. Didn't anyone have an ounce of compassion left in them?

Nearly twenty minutes later, she stalked barefoot and seething to the kitchen where Cherry was pouring two mugs of coffee. She set them on the dinette table—Frankie winced as she looked at it—where there was already a bowl of steaming chicken noodle soup and what looked to be a tuna salad sandwich.

"Sit."

Frankie crossed her arms and glared. "Don't boss me around, Cherry. Everyone else lets you get away with it, but don't try it with me."

"Then act like the Frankie Jones I used to know." Cherry pointed to Honey's cage, and then the screen door where Maury, Callie, Buck and Rasputin peered in hopefully. "When was the last time you took the cover off that bird's cage except to feed it? When was the last time you took care of those poor beasts out there?"

"I've been feeding them!"

"You know what I mean. They need more than food. They need attention. Love. Those are your words, Frankie."

She was right. Frankie cringed inside, realizing that in her self-pity she'd been turning her back on everyone, everything around her. She looked at the screen door, touched her hand to it. Immediately Maury and the others clamored over each other to lick at her palm.

"Hello, babies." After several seconds of cooing, she turned back to Cherry and grimaced. "I'm sorry."

"Sit down and eat and maybe I'll forgive you. You look like the breeze from that fan will knock you over."

"In a minute." Instead she went to Honey's cage and not only removed the cover, she opened the door. Then she picked up Dr. J., lying listlessly in a corner. "Bet you're tired of being cooped up, huh? How about a little sunshine?"

After letting him out, she passed the bookcase where she reached up to scratch Bugsy under his chin. He opened and shut his mouth as if trying to return her greeting.

She washed her hands, then transferred the food Cherry had prepared to the counter. "I can't sit there," she told her friend.

"Fine. Whatever, as long as you eat." Cherry, too, moved her coffee and settled on the bar stool beside her. She watched like the proverbial hawk, until Frankie made a serious attempt at ingesting the soup. "Have you seen a paper since all this happened?"

"I don't want to discuss it."

"I know you never replaced the TV that died, but how about the radio news?"

"This is good soup."

"That's what I figured, which is why I brought these." Cherry reached into her bag she'd retrieved from the bedroom while Frankie had been showering, and drew out a handful of press clippings. "Most of it's repeat stuff, because he's apparently a pretty private guy, but you'll get a basic idea about who he is. Read them," Cherry said, nodding as she dropped them on the counter. "They'll let you see that you're mourning someone who doesn't exist. It may help you put this behind you and get on with your life."

What was she talking about? Granted, Johnny Shepherd may not have been a legitimate name, but the man who'd used it was every bit as real as she was. No matter what Cherry tried to insist, she wouldn't stop believing that. Nevertheless, she didn't touch the pile of clippings, either.

"His name is Ranier John Sullivan," Cherry began reciting.

"I *know* what his name is."

"He's thirty-five, was born and raised in Chicago—when he wasn't overseas in one school or another. He has a string of degrees so long." Cherry measured with her hands a yard apart. "Smart cookie, apparently. And filthy rich."

Thirty-five. Frankie remembered his concern about their ages and felt a bittersweet pang. Thirty-five wasn't old at all.

"Comes from old money. You know, the *really* rich who never show up in society columns or do interviews? And apparently he's managed to more than double the family's wealth since his father's death. He's quite the investment whiz, your R.J."

"He's not *my* R.J. He's not my anything."

"Including that teddy bear I told you he wasn't. I was right about that, sugar."

"Congratulations. Have half of this sandwich. I'm all out of trophies," Frankie muttered, shoving the plate toward her. Maybe if she filled her mouth with food, Cherry would stop talking.

"They say he's one of the shrewdest, most cold-blooded businessmen around," Cherry continued, as if she hadn't spoken. "He supposedly once drove a former classmate into bankruptcy, and they say he didn't attend his own father's funeral."

"Cherry, stop it."

"I'm not making anything up. It's all in there," she said, nodding to the clippings.

"It doesn't matter. Don't you get it? It done. Over."

"But you fell in love with him."

She'd fallen in love with an image she helped create. An image that was no more hers to keep than R.J. Sullivan—a big shark in the financial waters of the world—was hers to understand, let alone love. Yes, it was ironic that his middle name was John; but apparently no one called him that. *No one* called him Johnny.

Now she knew why her gramps had taken to the road when her grandmother died. Staying put where the memories were had proved too much for him. Her memories were too much for her. But she couldn't uproot herself because she had other responsibilities . . . Lambchop. George. Rasputin. The others might be all right if she relocated, but not those dear souls. She had to stay for their sake.

"I'll be at work tonight," she told her friend. "That is, if I still have a job?"

"Don't be a pea brain. You know Benny wants you back. He feels responsible for this in a way. If it wasn't for Deke, the authorities would never have been called in and Johnny—R.J.— would never have been found."

Frankie shook her head. "You know that's silly. He would have remembered eventually. In fact there were moments when I saw a certain expression in his eyes. . . ." She shivered. "No doubt he has total recall already."

"What he hasn't regained is any sense of decency or manners," Cherry muttered, scowling. "He lived off you for days. You'd think he might have sent you something for all you've done for him. Flowers. Something."

"I don't want anything. I did what I did because it was the right thing to do."

"Including sleeping with the guy? Men like that usually give their mistresses costly little trinkets when they kiss them goodbye. All you got out of it is a few more T-shirts to add to your wardrobe."

Damn Cherry for bringing up a brief, earlier conversation. Not wanting to respond to that, Frankie asked, "Did you hear if the authorities have figured out what happened to him?"

"Nope. Other than the fact they think he was mugged while on a business trip down here."

Frankie eyed the clippings. "Leave them." She would read everything and then maybe she would be able to exorcise Johnny Shepherd from her head and her heart once and for all.

Apparently she looked better, because Cherry nodded with approval. "Good girl. I'll leave you to it, then. Oh, one thing that may cause you a little concern. Not concern, really. Embarrassment? Benny asked Stan to come back. Deke's been transported back to prison in Minnesota for violating his parole, and Benny was concerned that Stan would lose heart, being alone and all."

"That's nice. He was right to ask his friend back. It's not Stan's fault that his nephew chose to be a jerk."

She walked Cherry to her car, lifting Buck into her arms, and petting the others as they herded around her. They sensed the change in her. She sensed it in herself. Just in time, too—her yard was beginning to look like a jungle, despite Rasputin's and Lambchop's grazing.

"See you tonight," she called, then waved as Cherry pulled away.

Frankie drew a deep breath and looked up at the sky. She didn't feel good by any means, but she felt better. Functional. Even the sound of a tractor in the distance brought a bittersweet smile. Mr. Miller was working in one of his pastures. The sound reminded her of the conversation they'd had after Johnny left.

"Brought your mail, sunshine. Where's your fella?"

Her throat so raw she could barely get the words out, she'd said, "He had to go, Mr. Miller. His . . . vacation was over."

"Vacation? I never knew he was on just a vacation. Well, I wanted him to have a good laugh at my expense. Remember I told you he reminded me of somebody? I found the picture."

He'd passed it over. It was a television advertisement, a scene from a new film based on a bestselling thriller. The actor was a household name, as famous for his romantic-comedy roles as for his dramatic work.

"Yes, I see the similarity," she'd said, remembering how Johnny had worried that Mr. Miller recognized him from a Wanted poster or something. She smiled sadly and handed it back.

"Naw, you keep it. You can show him the next time you see him. He might get a kick out of it."

"Sure," Frankie had said, feeling the unshed tears burning like acid behind her eyes.

"Next time," she murmured, heading back inside. Now, there was something really funny.

"Give it some time, R.J."

Damn it, he didn't have time! Didn't anyone get that?

Every hour, every day he spent up here, was one more day of feeling Frankie slipping out of reach. There wasn't time!

"I know you think that now that you've begun to remember things—"

"I remember everything," R.J. snapped at Sid Birnbaum across the span of his desk. "All of it."

"Then that's all the more reason not to rush things." With a sigh, Sid slipped off his glasses and pinched the bridge of his nose. "Hell, why do I put myself through this? You don't care what I think."

R.J. understood the dark-haired man's frustration. They'd known each other since college. Both had played on the school's tennis and golf teams. Sid had gone on to get his medical degree and was an up-and-coming partner in one of the most successful clinics in the city. While R.J. didn't call anyone friend, Sid came closest to being one. The two played golf together once or twice a week, and the few times that R.J. had asked for advice or help in his life, Sid had been the one he called.

There was, however, a price to be paid for being a confidant of R.J. Sullivan, and Sid was paying it by dealing with R.J.'s scorn whenever Sid said something R.J. didn't like. "I know you think I'm being a royal pain with my appeal to be conservative, however, I'm not speaking merely as your doctor, but as your friend. You not only suffered a major trauma a few weeks ago, it stirred one hell of a hornet's nest in your psyche. Any radical decision you make now before you've given yourself sufficient opportunity to reconcile the past with the present could have a devastating effect on your future. Would that be fair to any of the parties involved?"

There was only *one* party he cared about at this stage. In the several days since he'd returned to Chicago, he'd lived in a kind of purgatory, worrying about her, hurting for her, for what she might be going through, and fearing that she would vanish on him before he could get things—his life, as well as ghosts from the past and a few bloodsuckers in the present—straightened out. She represented his sanity; his opportunity to have a real, *sane* life. If anyone was supposed to understand what that meant to him, it was Sid.

"I do understand," Sid replied, when R.J. said as much to him. "Believe me, I've done nothing but listen to you since your return. I'm delighted you finally stopped blocking out that you come from a textbook dysfunctional family, and that you had a father that would make Mr. Hyde sound like a cupcake. I'm glad that we've begun to unlock a good number of doors regarding your childhood trauma, and that you're coming to terms with why most people see you as a ruthless SOB, including your brother." Sid replaced his glasses and eyed his friend dourly. "But if I let you, you could still scare the pants off me. From what you've told me about her, do you honestly think your tenderhearted Frankie could survive a carnivore like you?"

"I've changed. She changed me."

Sid inclined his head, his dark, intelligent gaze reflective. "Something is different about you. But to what degree it's the woman, who can say? It could also be a result of the attack you suffered, although the tests we ran show no lasting damage beyond some bruising. For all I know you were touched by an angel, had an out-of-body experience, or met up with aliens."

R.J. ignored Sid's sarcasm to focus on the only thing of importance he'd said. "She's not 'the woman.' Her name is Frankie."

"I remember... but do you remember that when I arrived a few minutes ago, I witnessed Greta running out of here crying her heart out? If that's an example of how you treat women—"

"Greta doesn't have a heart, she has a platinum credit card in her chest. That performance was for your benefit, just as everything else she's done since bringing me home has been an act. She belongs on stage, and the only reason she isn't is because being a Sullivan has proved more lucrative."

That stunt she'd pulled by flying down to Texas had cinched it for him. Up until then he'd tolerated the conniving witch for Collin's sake, but no more. If his brother wanted to let his wife play him for a fool while she baited more lucrative Sullivan waters, that was his business; for R.J.'s part, he might not be able to take away her name, but he could sure get her out of his sight.

"As for Frankie," he continued, aware of the ache the mere mention of her name caused him, "whether you believe me or not, I would never subject her to that person I was."

"You think 'that person' is gone? And don't you think she's read or heard enough about you at this point to realize she's had a close call and is lucky to have escaped? She would take one look at you sitting there right now, and run in terror. That blank look is gone from your eyes, R.J. Like it or not, the ruthlessness and killer instinct your father drilled into you is back. I'm not sure you'll ever be able to erase it from your psyche. If she's only a fraction of the person you described, you won't be able to hide that from her. She'll sense it."

"I'll take my chances."

"Damn you. I'm asking you to have pity on her. I'll beg if that's what it takes. You need months more of therapy before we get to the bottom of who you are and what damage the old man did to you. Someday—"

"No, now. She's mine," R.J. said with a sense of grim finality. Then he sighed. "And I'm hers. She's the only therapy I need. I don't expect you to understand, or approve, Sid. I just know that if I lose her... I can't accept that as a possibility. I won't.''

Another day passed, and another, then a few more. Frankie discovered that she'd been wrong initially; survival *was* easier when you moved on and rejoined the world at large.

She went back to work. Since the nights were the worst, it helped to have The Two-Step and her friends there to keep her preoccupied. And her animals helped the rest of the time. They kept her busy, and offered a love that touched her heart. Sometimes she was certain they knew what she was enduring, that they missed Johnny themselves.

It was primarily the early hours of the morning that created the worst strain on her nerves, and her body. Memories of making love with him, the whispers, the tenderness... they all came back then with a vengeance. She was lucky she didn't need a great deal of sleep, or else her health would have been threatened by now. But that wasn't to say she was all right.

Mentally, she was having difficulty coping with more than losing Johnny; she had to accept that if by some miracle R.J. Sullivan showed up on her doorstep, there could be nothing between them—and not just because he was married.

She'd read Cherry's clippings, and at The Two-Step just about everyone knew her story. People seemed to think it was their civic duty to keep a vigilant eye on the papers and present her with anything that came up regarding Ranier John Sullivan. Admittedly there was little and nothing about his wife, which spoke volumes as to the wealth and power of the Sullivan name, but what there was had been a death knell for the innocence in the sweet love she'd felt for him.

The man was recognized in the financial community as a predator, and while respected—not to mention envied—he wasn't exactly well-liked. The one or two file photos run on him were a few years old. Both the posed and candid shot exposed a grim-faced, cold-eyed mogul who quite honestly made her uneasy.

Not in a million years would R.J. Sullivan be caught helping her move a big old snapping turtle out of the road because she'd been concerned someone might run over it as Johnny had.

Not in two million would he help her take Callie, Maury and Buck to the nursing home in town so they could cheer up the lonely residents. But Johnny did, and she'd never caught him eyeing a clock once.

Not for anything would R.J. risk a rabies bite and the loss of a full night's sleep to stand guard outside and chase away a pack of coyotes from George and his pond. Johnny hadn't hesitated.

In his own way, Johnny Shepherd had died. What they'd shared was a fleeting blip in time, an accident destiny had corrected as soon as it realized its error. Theirs had been just another love story. Nothing as special and rare as she'd let herself believe. Never meant to last.

She was thinking all that as she stood in the ladies' room digging in her purse for her brush and came across an article instead. It was the first Saturday in August and the club had closed for the night. Frankie quickly perused the thing, realizing it was one Holly had given her that she'd shoved in her purse and hadn't read.

The door swung open and Cherry appeared. She took one look at the crumpled clipping and fumed. "You said you weren't reading those anymore! The only reason I gave you the ones I did was to wisen you up."

"It's an old one. I forgot it was in here."

"Sure, sure." Cherry snatched it from her, crushed it between both hands and tossed it into the trash. "Now it's really gone."

It amazed Frankie how strong the impulse was to dive in after it. "Fine," she said weakly.

"Fine," Cherry mimicked. "You're telling yourself you should forget him, but your heart isn't listening to your head, is it?"

"I'm getting there."

"Let me tell you something," the waitress continued as if Frankie hadn't spoken, "it better start or you're going to bleed to death over someone who's already forgotten you."

"Thank you, Cherry."

"I'm not trying to be cruel, sweet pea. It's just killing me to see someone as special as you get your heart trampled by someone who probably eats steak tartare three times a day. Probably fresh cut off his staff!"

"You can be so gruesome." And despite knowing it would invite Cherry's ire, she still couldn't help pointing out, "He wasn't like that with me."

"He wasn't *himself* with you. He was out of his mind. He had amnesia, for pity's sake. But now he's back to his old self. Most important—he's *married!* You said it yourself. Let him go."

Exasperated, Frankie abandoned the idea of brushing her hair and braided it instead. Throwing her just-found brush back into her bag, she snapped, "You know, Cherry, I'd love to. But it would help if everyone stopped bringing him up!"

Naturally, by the time she left the club and headed for Petunia, she felt like a shrew. She would have done an about-face, and apologized, if she wasn't so tired. Thank goodness she knew the route so well, she could almost make the trip home blindfolded.

She was on the other side of the interstate, thinking about making Cherry the peach ice cream she loved so as a peace offering, when Petunia began coughing. It wasn't an I'm-out-of-gas cough, either, although she'd been known to get so preoccupied that it occasionally happened.

Could it be that Petunia had finally had it? "No!" Frankie cried as the truck began to slow... and rolled to a stop. "Your timing stinks!"

She eyed the area and gauged she was only about a quarter of a mile from home. Not far at all to walk, except that it was almost two in the morning and a person would have to be suicidal to walk alone at this hour, particularly a woman. On the other hand, it was rare to meet anyone on this road at this hour. She definitely didn't relish spending the night in Petunia, whose seat springs were more shot than her engine.

The animals would be upset if she didn't return, too.

She started walking. The night sounds were wild, but familiar. She didn't mind them. Besides, she had plenty to think about, like what she should shop for in transportation come morning if she could get Mr. Miller to take her to town, and how big a dip she would have to make into her savings. So preoccupied was she that she was late to hear the vehicle coming up behind her. Wondering why she hadn't been warned by headlights or even flashes of the high beams, she spun around, nearly twisting her ankle.

The driver had shut off his headlights and was driving with only his parking lights!

Frankie stared as the limousine purred to a stop beside her. The rear window eased down.

"Oh, my God," she breathed.

Ten

"Get in."

The words came out sharp and hard-edged, even to his own ears. That wasn't his intention, but between the long trip and the condition of his nerves of late, he wasn't in as much control of himself as he would like. Seeing Petunia abandoned back there hadn't helped, either. But most of all he didn't like the shock and panic he saw in her eyes as she stared at him now.

"Frankie," he said, more quietly.

"This isn't real. This can't be happening. I must be losing my mind...."

Between her barely audible whispers and his relief at seeing her safe, his reaction overrode wisdom. "You have to be to be walking home at this hour in the middle of nowhere. My God, woman, after what you've been through lately? I should—" Fighting back his own terror for her, he thrust open the door. "Get in."

She didn't. Instead she backed away, the strangest look coming over her face.

"What do you think you're doing?"

"Go away."

"Francesca!"

She ran. He couldn't believe it. She was running away from him?

He slammed the door shut and leaned forward. "Go after her," he ordered the chauffeur.

Fortunately, they weren't that far from the trailer; otherwise, it would have been unbearable to watch—her racing, frantic like a gazelle as the driver turned on the limousine's headlights; unable to escape her predator. That's why he'd ordered the headlights off in the first place—to avoid startling her, to signal her that it was him. He'd told her he would be back! But she hadn't understood any of that; what could he do but keep after her until he could explain?

"I said *follow* her!"

"Mr. Sullivan, sir," the driver replied over his shoulder, "I don't feel good about this."

R.J. couldn't remember the man's name. The limousine had been arranged for by his staff to meet him in Houston where he'd landed. And he didn't have time for lengthy explanations. Reaching into his billfold he tossed a few bills over the seat. "Just let me out and go find yourself a motel. Come back with my luggage in the morning. You'll locate the trailer just down the road."

"Are you sure about this, sir?"

But R.J. had already climbed out and slammed the door, no longer interested in anything the man had to say. He was concerned that Frankie would escape into the trailer and lock him out. As it was, he could tell his greatest fears had come true: she'd seen or read too much about him in the news.

The limo already forgotten, he took off after her. She had a considerable head start, but he'd gone back to his exercise program since returning to Chicago, and it wasn't long before he followed her over the cattle guard and down the dirt drive.

Already confused by her odd arrival, Maury provided an immediate challenge, growling a warning and assuming a stance that was quickly duplicated by young Buck the moment they spotted him. More unsettling was seeing Frankie pass the trailer altogether and keep on running!

"Hey—good boy...good dogs. Damn it, don't you two remember me?"

His voice did have some effect on them, but he still had to stop or risk getting attacked. It was Lambchop, however, who stretched to nuzzle his suit pocket in search of a treat. He could only imagine what her drool would do to the fine fabric. Then again, he didn't care. Her acceptance intrigued Buck, who waddled closer to sniff his Italian loafers and then yelped excitedly. And that finally won over Maury.

"Finally," he muttered, patting all three quickly and taking off again. "You guys *stay!*"

By the time he neared the dock by the pond, he was sweating like a long-distance runner and flung off the jacket.

Somewhere beyond it, he ripped off his tie.

By the time he was in the meadow, he began gaining on her, but his silk shirt felt as constricting as a straitjacket. He tore at the buttons.

Despite years of regular workouts in his private gym, he had to push with everything he had to catch her, especially after she dropped her canvas shoulder bag. When the moon outlined the woods ahead, he knew that if she reached them, he might never find her, and so with the stars watching like a million judgmental eyes, he lunged the last yards separating them and took her down.

Her scream broke his heart. Not even in his most fearful scenarios had he imagined things going like this. But then touching her again became his salvation.

"Frankie," he gasped, fighting for breath, let alone the right words to appeal to her to listen so he could make it all right. He literally dragged himself over her, like a soldier inching through a minefield, while she lay facedown in the grass, sobbing. "Baby, don't."

She cried harder.

He stroked her hair, rolled her over to lift her into his arms. She felt so good, he shook with reaction. Surely, surely, if she felt how badly he needed this, she would listen, understand what he'd been trying to do.

"L-let me go. I can't bear it . . . p-please!"

Couldn't bear what? His touch? The thought, as much as her fists pushing at his chest to free herself, brought a pain he'd never known, not even when he'd left her. She was killing him.

Her rejection sapped his strength, and his arms fell limp at his sides. "Frankie . . . you don't mean that. I came back just like I promised."

Free, she scampered on all fours until she was a few feet away from him and turned to glare, wary and accusing. "You shouldn't have."

"Why not?"

"You're *married!*"

That was it? He could have thrown back his head and laughed in relief, except that his desire to strangle Greta was still strong; stronger now than during their last confrontation a few hours ago.

"I'm not."

"I saw her!"

"You saw my brother's wife."

Her mouth fell open. That wonderful, delectable mouth that he'd dreamed about these past nights to keep himself sane.

"Your... brother?"

"I have a brother. His name is Collin. He's six years younger, and for the most part we grew up separately."

He waited for her to take that in, to make some comment. She simply hovered there, unsure and hurting.

Of course, she is, you fool. You haven't told her anything yet compared to what she's learned through hearsay.

"I'm not married." Her expression in the moonlight told him she didn't know whether to believe him or not. This time he understood. "You're wondering why another man's wife would leave her husband to come after her brother-in-law. Yes, well, I suppose you'd have to spend some time around her to really catch on."

"I didn't like her," Frankie allowed. "But you said you'd seen her in your dreams."

R.J. nodded his approval of her opinion, as well as his understanding. "More like my nightmares, so you can imagine what I thought when I first saw her. Even without my memory back, something didn't feel right. She's a calculating bitch and always plotting her next coup. In this case it happened to be me." It was a long, insane story. His entire life was that. How on earth could he hope to make Frankie understand a fraction of it?

His breath beginning to come easier, R.J. sat back on his heels and tried to capsulize for her. "Greta met Collin while he was on a business trip for me. She's a fast operator, and by the time he returned to Chicago, he had more than the contract I'd sent him out to get. Once Greta realized there were bigger fish in the proverbial Sullivan pond, she let it be known she wouldn't mind making some minor adjustments to her monogrammed stationery. She's been trying to make a play for me ever since."

"That's... psychotic!"

"To try to take advantage of your husband's brother while he didn't know who he was? Yes, it was a new low even for her. But then, where money and power are concerned, Greta never did have much of a conscience."

"Does your brother know about her?"

"He does now. And he did before in a way, but he thought he was in love. Discovering Greta's duplicity, how she hired her own private detective to search for me, and had kept the phone call from the sheriff a secret, hoping to get to me first and arrange something compromising... well, that cured him." R.J. had felt a surprising compassion for him when they'd finally spoken about it earlier today. But that was because he knew about love. Now.

"What he does about her is his business," he continued with a fatalistic shrug. He could tell Frankie thought that was a bit cold-blooded, and he took a deep breath, appealing to her with the tenderness she'd taught him so well. "What I'm trying to say is that I've helped him all I can. The final decision about what to do with his life is his. As for me—there's no one. Not anyone, but you. That's why I'm here, angel. For you."

She wanted to believe him; he saw it in the way her eyes grew soft and shimmered, the way she pressed her clasped hands to her lips as if in prayer. But something held her back. "What?" he coaxed, determined to be patient, no matter what it cost him.

"But... you're different. The articles. What everybody writes about you. The way you looked at me back in that limousine. And just—that limousine!"

On impulse he stripped off his already unbuttoned dress shirt. "No. Not that different. Not impossibly different. There are the trappings, and there was the man I was, the role I played because it was all I knew, because it was a way to survive, true. But look..." He cast away the shirt without so much as a look. "None of that matters. It's who I am inside. Who I became when you found me and took me into your home and your heart." He spread his arms, inviting her. "Who do you see?"

She looked heartbreakingly lovely, gossamer in the moonlight, and he needed to touch her. She had no idea how much. But he waited, knowing how much their future depended on it.

Then she flung herself into his arms. Thank God, he thought, locking his arms around her. Thank God. If she hadn't—

No, he didn't have to think like a desperate man anymore. His days as a predator were done.

Knee to knee, shoulder to shoulder, and every part in between, he crushed her closer and sought her mouth to kiss her the way he'd been dying to since the moment their world turned inside out.

They both uttered soul-deep sounds at the joining. Their bodies shook from the release of emotions too long restrained. With their first kiss he telegraphed to her how miserable he'd been since leaving Texas; how he'd burned with fever and ached with need at the merest thought of her; it would have taken handcuffs now to keep from exploring her again.

He filled his hands with her wonderful hair, wrapped it around them as the kiss went on. It smelled like a wildflower meadow and dreams, and the only reason he abandoned it was to drive his hands into its lush depths to cup her head and turn the kiss into a promise.

When he slid his hands down the length of her small back, to her incredible waist and her sleek hips, he noted her more fragile shape, and it delivered a punch to his heart. She'd missed him, suffered. Because of him. How he wished he could have spared her the doubts. But he knew he could give her all their tomorrows.

The grass became their bed; moonlit daisies became their pillow. As R.J. slowly bared her for his eyes, his hands, his mouth, he thought she'd never looked more lovely, more precious. She was his heart. Proving that became as important as it was natural. He loved her until her skin took on the dewy gleam of pearls...until his tender touch had her weeping for him...until he'd driven her to one climax with his hands, and another with his mouth. Only then did he allow himself to open his own clothes and find his home in her incredible heat.

"Johnny..."

The voice he would have sacrificed anything he owned to hear again. The name that represented his rebirth. She'd given him his dream.

"I love you. I love you," he whispered, and they were words he rasped over and over, until she crested again and carried him with her to heaven.

They had to be crazy, Frankie thought. Making love in the middle of a pasture, in the middle of the night when who knew what they could have tripped over—what could trip over them! The fact that Maury and the others hadn't chased after them was a miracle in its own right.

Oh, but she'd never felt more glorious or alive!

This was the craziest thing *she'd* ever done. Well, next to picking a naked man up in the middle of the night. Frankie grinned to herself as she remembered.

"I felt that," he murmured into her hair. "What's going on in that delectable mind of yours?"

She took hold of his head and forced him to rise so she could see his face. "Who are you?" she demanded, even as he continued to throb inside her.

"The man who isn't complete without you. Johnny to you. Sullivan, not Shepherd, I'm afraid, but everything else is the same." He took hold of one hand and planted a tender kiss at her wrist and then into her palm.

Yes, this was the man she'd been missing. She touched his firm, sensual mouth, his strong straight nose, his almost-healed brow. She looked for any coldness, remoteness lingering in his eyes and found none. Only adoration. Only love.

"I'm sorry for frightening you half to death, angel."

She was more than willing to forgive him, but she wanted him to understand what she'd been feeling. "At first I couldn't believe it was you. Then I was afraid. If you were back to being the man in the newspaper photographs, then there was no hope for us."

"I know. I used to be an angry man. But Frankie, there were reasons. Things that happened in my past I need to share with you, and then maybe you'll never be afraid again."

"So the reports were right? You remember now?"

"About my life before coming here? Almost everything. Regarding the attack, not much, and the doctors have told me that I might never regain that block of time between knowing I was on the interstate, then seeing you for the first time.

"But the police have deduced from the information they were able to collect and what testimony I gave them, that it wasn't premeditated. I was simply in the wrong place at the wrong time."

Although Frankie couldn't repress a shiver as she thought how it could have turned out so much worse, she said, "I read that this area was never a part of the investigation circle because your rental car had been found in New Orleans."

"I have business dealings there, as well, and they assumed I'd changed my itinerary after Houston. What complicated things was that for several days the Houston people were unavailable to contradict that, which caused even more of a delay in adjusting the police's theory."

What a strange turn of events. Frankie sighed thinking of what else she'd read. "Does it bother you to know that they're doubtful the perpetrators will ever be apprehended?"

"Not really. I'm learning that fate has a way of dealing with justice itself."

"I don't know that I'm feeling as generous," she admitted, frowning. "But I am grateful that you were so lucky."

"Heaven sent me an angel."

Had she been directed to him to change his life? What a wonderful thought. How much did he intend to change hers? For how long? A few days? Weeks?

"Johnny, how long can you stay?"

The question clearly startled him. "You don't get it, do you?" he murmured incredulously.

When she shook her head to signal the negative, he smiled. A moment later he was sitting up and had her on his lap.

"Let me finish telling you everything. Maybe then you'll be able to answer your own question."

As impatient as she was, she did want to understand. "Will you start by telling me what the doctors said about your reluctance to go to the police or even to get medical help?"

"Mmm. It would seem past trauma got tangled with present trauma and created its own scenario."

"Your nightmares," she whispered. Dear heaven, what did he mean by past trauma? She didn't want to know if he'd done something terrible. She didn't think she could bear that.

When she voiced that fear, Johnny became instantly reassuring. "Frankie, seeing myself as a boy locked in darkness was literal. It happened to me. Often. And there was more. I didn't have a ... normal childhood. My father was a hard man. I'm not sure I'll ever fully understand what drove him, but besides being ambitious, he was obsessed with not letting anyone find a weakness in him. Some of it had to do with the fact that he had his own painful memories. His father's failure as a businessman and subsequent suicide, for one. He was determined that wouldn't be the case for him or his son."

"He beat you?"

"Sometimes. More often than not, though, he would lock me in a closet in a remote part of the house to toughen me up."

With a shudder, Frankie wrapped her arms around his neck. That explained why he'd become upset at the idea of being closed in her shower stall. "What a hideous man. How did you bear it?"

"Not well, apparently."

He told her that he did, however, succeed in protecting his younger brother, Collin, who undoubtedly would have suffered an equally harsh childhood if he hadn't intervened.

"Where was your mother in all this?"

"Standing by virtually helpless. You have to realize that my father was wealthy and powerful. He warned her that if she tried to interfere by going to the authorities, he would see she was reduced to a laughingstock. He would've thrown her out and she would've lost both of her sons. So I convinced her to leave and take Collin with her. He was barely five, and my father had struck him for the first time."

"You sacrificed your own happiness for his," she whispered, stunned by the courage and strength he must have had even as a boy.

"Yes, but don't give me undeserved credit. As much as I wanted to spare my brother the grief I'd known, I did it to spite my father first and foremost."

"You did become hard and ruthless, but not for the reasons he wanted."

"Exactly. My intention was to survive him in order to destroy him."

"And did you?"

"No. He died of a stroke several years ago. So I tried to get back at him, prove something, by becoming more powerful, more successful than he'd been. It didn't seem to matter to me that people saw me as a chip off the old block, as bad as he'd been. By the time I realized how wrong I was, I was trapped in my own vicious cycle."

He gazed deeply into her eyes. "Then I was nearly murdered and met you. You showed me that there was more to life than revenge, that I wasn't a prisoner of my anger and bitterness. You proved there was a kernel of decency left in me."

"Johnny, there's more than a kernel. Much more." She hugged him tightly willing him to believe it. "And you showed incredible bravery and wisdom for someone so young. Does Collin know all this?"

"Yes. We've been talking since my return to Chicago. But words aren't the same as actually living through what I have. He remains more afraid of me than grateful. I suppose that's partly my fault for not always letting my actions back up my words. Sorry, love," he murmured, kissing her again.

"I guess there are plenty of rough edges left for you to smooth out."

"Not many," Frankie murmured against his lips. And she proved it by coaxing him into showing her another measure of how gentle and caring he could be.

They didn't speak again for a long while. When she caught her breath again, she asked, "What happened to your mother?"

"She's remarried. Happily, this time. I see her over the holidays. We had our problems earlier on when I belatedly discovered I resented her leaving me behind, but we're finding our way back." He told her how for a while he'd believed she was the other woman in his dreams, but that thanks to Sid's help, he had determined the woman had been involved with the muggings.

His was a compelling and tragic story, and now that he'd told her, she could identify moments when she'd glimpsed the frightened little boy he'd been, the boy who'd never learned to laugh freely and play. That could be her gift to him, if he would let her.

"One thing you're wrong about," she told him, brushing his mussed hair off his forehead. "I still don't know how long you can stay."

With a wicked glimmer in his eyes, he coaxed her back into his arms and kissed her breast. "Think about it. I didn't use anything to protect you a few minutes ago. What would you say if you discovered I'd made you pregnant?"

She studied him in the darkness. His was the face she adored, would always adore, and the thought of carrying his child filled her with a happiness that was at once giddy and awesome. But...

"Are you sure?"

It was his turn to grow somber. "Don't you love me?"

"Johnny, every day without you has been its own nightmare. And I worried about you so, wondering if you'd regained your memory, if you were happy. If your *wife* was being good to you," she added with a rueful grimace. "What was she doing in your dreams?"

"Believe me, I didn't want her there. I suppose my subconscious was trying to deal with what she was doing to my brother and how to tell him. In a way she represented as much of a threat to what I wanted with you as my father did."

That made sense to Frankie, and she was relieved it wasn't what she'd feared.

"Hmm . . . I think I like inciting a little jealousy in you."

"There was nothing little about it."

His grin was wide and confident in the moonlight—but fleeting. Serious again, he tilted her face toward his. "Then why do you resist telling me what I've been waiting to hear? Say it, Frankie. Give me the words I need to make me whole."

"I love you."

He stroked her lower lip with his thumb. "And now, 'Yes, I'll marry you, Johnny.'"

His gentle teasing made her press her face against his shoulder to hide her grin. "I think there may be a bit of the dictator left in you that I won't be able to get rid of."

"You don't want to. He's the one who broke through both of our defenses that last night...and who thought you were more delectable than food at the kitchen table the next morning."

A hot flush swept over her as she remembered that. "I get the picture."

With a happy sigh, she sat up. That's when she looked over his shoulder and saw Buck crawling toward them on his belly; and Maury not far behind, his ears back flat, eagerly hoping for a sign of welcome.

"Oh, Johnny, look. Aren't they adorable? Tell me I'm not going to have to give up my animals."

He did look and pretended to think about that, long and hard. Then he shrugged. "Why don't I build you a bigger house and a nice big barn so you can get more?"

"Johnny!"

The force of her hug sent him rolling onto his back and she smothered him with kisses. Their laughter was lighter and more carefree than ever before.

"Tomorrow when the chauffeur comes back with my luggage, we'll go see your Mr. Miller and talk to him about buying this place."

"He's lived here all his life. I'm not sure he'll want to sell."

"He can stay on for as long as he wants. I just want to build a place for you."

She didn't know whether to laugh or cry. "But what about you? Could you be happy here?"

"If you're with me, I could live in an igloo."

She was beginning to believe him. Already she could see a serene light in his eyes again, the lines ease around his eyes and mouth. "And what will you do way out here in the middle of nowhere?"

"Enjoy what being in love is all about. Spend some of the money I've been accumulating over the years. That's never appealed to me before. Having fun...learning to play." He shrugged. "Eventually find something constructive to do with my brain." Cupping her cheek, he kissed her. "Does any of that scare you? Having me around so much? Wanting to be with you? Spoil you a little? Does it sound too obsessive or possessive?"

"No," she replied, her heart feeling so full at that admission and his sweet concern. "It sounds perfect. More than I ever dreamed we could have."

"Then time's up. Say it. Say, 'I'll marry you, Johnny.'"

"I want to give you babies, Johnny."

"Close enough," he murmured, taking her back with him to mingle with the daisies once more.

Frankie laughed in delight and pleasure, and from only yards away came Maury's and Buck's excited barks and yelps, then Callie's approving meow. From farther back she heard Lambchop's whinny and Rasputin's bray, and even a snort or two from Samson.

It seemed the entire family approved of their plan.

Epilogue

He couldn't find her. He'd checked the whole house, and rang the phone in the barn, but there wasn't a sign of her anywhere. Johnny told himself not to panic, that there was a simple explanation, but nevertheless, the knot formed in his stomach. It always did when she was out of his sight for too long.

He loved her so much. More than his own life. If something happened to her...

He paused by their wedding photograph on the table by the picture window that looked out over the pond. They'd been married in September, the earliest they could get both families together. Arranging that had almost tempted him to kidnap Frankie and elope. But it had been worth it—meeting his new family, introducing her to Collin and his mother, who immediately fell in love with her.

The house had taken a bit longer because they'd wanted something special to complement their unique life-style, yet flatter the scenic East Texas landscape. Designed with natural stone as well as cedar beams, and enhanced with panoramic windows, it was proving to be a perfect nest for their ever-deepening love.

But his little bird had flown the coop, damn it. Didn't she know that drove him nuts, particularly at this delicate time?

The sound of an approaching tractor had him bolting outside. Even before he rounded to the back of the house, he could hear Maury and a much-grown Buck barking their greeting. That made him feel better, because they never let Frankie too far out of their sight.

But when he saw old Mr. Miller towing his utility trailer behind him, and that Buck and Maury joined a reclining Frankie in the bed of the thing, his heart leaped to his throat.

"What's happened?" he demanded, racing to her side. "What's wrong?"

"Now don't scold, Johnny," Frankie replied soothingly as she cradled her swollen stomach. "I was just out walking to check on that family of beavers by the creek. You know they've been washed out of their home twice now, due to our heavy June rains, and I wanted to be sure they were all right."

And what did she think she could do about it, especially in her condition? Rebuild the dam for them? Groaning, he raked his hand through his hair. "Frankie...angel...I wish you'd tell me when you take off to do things like that. What if something happened? What if you went into labor while you were out there?"

"I did." She smiled. "I am. That's why I sent Maury to get Mr. Miller who was in the next pasture."

Johnny's heart went into overdrive again. Thank goodness the old farmer had been behaving much like her pets these days and keeping close tabs on her, too. He looked from her belly to her radiant face. "You mean it's *time?*"

From above them on the tractor, Mr. Miller shook his head. "Looks like I'm gonna have to do the driving to the hospital, too, Frankie. I don't think you'll be wanting to trust that fella behind a wheel."

Frankie laughed. "I think you're right, and I'm going to take you up on that, Mr. Miller." She extended one hand to Johnny. "Besides, I want *you* near *me.*"

No one could have gotten closer to her. He lifted her into his arms with as much care as if she were in the worst throes of labor, and carried her straight to the sedan. The moment he'd been dreaming about for months was about to come true. A child born out of their love was about to join them.

"Are you in pain? Are you scared? Can I do anything?" he asked in a rambling fashion that shocked even him.

"Mmm. You can stop panicking and go inside for my suitcase." But as he began to withdraw from the back seat, she grabbed the front of his shirt. "First, though, you can kiss me. The contractions aren't that close yet, and I don't think Johnny, Jr., will mind his mommy this one indulgence."

Her confidence and gentle teasing were the balm he needed to calm his nerves, and he kissed her with everything that was in his heart. "I adore you, Francesca Rose," he whispered when he found his voice again. "Thank you for showing me the possibilities."

"They're only beginning, love. They're only beginning."

* * * * *

COMING NEXT MONTH

It's Silhouette Desire's 1000th birthday! Join us for a spectacular three-month celebration, starring your favorite authors and the hottest heroes of the decade!

#991 SADDLE UP—Mary Lynn Baxter

One night with Bridget Martin had cost April's *Man of the Month*, single dad Jeremiah Davis, his bachelorhood! But would his new bride be the perfect mom for his little girl?

#992 THE GROOM, I PRESUME?—Annette Broadrick

Daughters of Texas

Maribeth O'Brien was everything Chris Cochran wanted in a woman. So when she was left at the altar by her delinquent groom, Chris stepped in and said, "I do"!

#993 FATHER OF THE BRAT—Elizabeth Bevarly

From Here to Paternity

Maddy Garrett had never liked arrogant Carver Venner. But now he needed her help—and Maddy couldn't resist his adorable daughter…or the sexy single dad!

#994 A STRANGER IN TEXAS—Lass Small

One passionate encounter with a handsome stranger had left Jessica Channing one very pregnant woman. Now the mysterious man was back, determined to discover Jessica's secret!

#995 FORGOTTEN VOWS—Modean Moon

The Wedding Night

Although Edward Carlton claimed his lovely bride had left him on their wedding night, Jennie didn't remember her husband. But she'd do anything to discover the truth about her past—and her marriage.…

#996 TWO WEDDINGS AND A BRIDE—Anne Eames

Debut Author

Brand-new bride Catherine Mason was furious when she caught her groom kissing her bridesmaid! So she went on her honeymoon with handsome Jake Alley—and hoped another wedding would soon be on the way.…

MILLION DOLLAR SWEEPSTAKES

It's time you joined...

MARIE FERRARELLA's

THE BABY OF THE MONTH CLUB

Silhouette Desire proudly presents *Husband: Optional,* book four of RITA Award-winning author Marie Ferrarella's miniseries, THE BABY OF THE MONTH CLUB, coming your way in March 1996.

She wasn't fooling him. Jackson Cain knew the baby Mallory Flannigan had borne was his...no matter that she *claimed* a conveniently absentee lover was Joshua's true dad. And though Jackson had left her once to "find" his true feelings, nothing was going to keep him away from this ready-made family now....

Do You Take This Child? We certainly hope you do, because in April 1996 Silhouette Romance will feature this final book in Marie Ferrarella's wonderful miniseries, THE BABY OF THE MONTH CLUB, found only in— Silhouette®

Bestselling author

RACHEL LEE

takes her Conard County series to new heights with

A Conard County Reckoning

This March, Rachel Lee brings readers a brand-new, longer-length, out-of-series title featuring the characters from her successful Conard County miniseries.

Janet Tate and Abel Pierce have both been betrayed and carry deep, bitter memories. Brought together by great passion, they must learn to trust again.

"Conard County is a wonderful place to visit! Rachel Lee has crafted warm, enchanting stories. These are wonderful books to curl up with and read. I highly recommend them."
—*New York Times* bestselling author
Heather Graham Pozzessere

Available in March, wherever Silhouette books are sold.

As seen on TV!
Free Gift Offer

With a Free Gift proof-of-purchase from any Silhouette® book,
you can receive a beautiful cubic zirconia pendant.

This gorgeous marquise-shaped stone is a genuine cubic
zirconia—accented by an 18" gold tone necklace.

(Approximate retail value $19.95)

Send for yours today...
compliments of ▼ *Silhouette*®
TM

To receive your free gift, a cubic zirconia pendant, send us one original proof-of-purchase, photocopies not accepted, from the back of any Silhouette Romance™, Silhouette Desire®, Silhouette Special Edition®, Silhouette Intimate Moments® or Silhouette Shadows™ title available in February, March or April at your favorite retail outlet, together with the Free Gift Certificate, plus a check or money order for $1.75 U.S./$2.25 CAN. (do not send cash) to cover postage and handling, payable to Silhouette Free Gift Offer. We will send you the specified gift. Allow 6 to 8 weeks for delivery. Offer good until April 30, 1996 or while quantities last. Offer valid in the U.S. and Canada only.

Free Gift Certificate

Name: _____

Address: _____

City: _____ State/Province: _____ Zip/Postal Code: _____

Mail this certificate, one proof-of-purchase and a check or money order for postage and handling to: SILHOUETTE FREE GIFT OFFER 1996. In the U.S.: 3010 Walden Avenue, P.O. Box 9057, Buffalo NY 14269-9057. In Canada: P.O. Box 622, Fort Erie,

---

FREE GIFT OFFER

ONE PROOF-OF-PURCHASE

079-KBZ-R

To collect your fabulous FREE GIFT, a cubic zirconia pendant, you must include this original proof-of-purchase for each gift with the properly completed Free Gift Certificate.

079-KBZ-R

SILHOUETTE... **Where Passion Lives**

Don't miss these Silhouette favorites by some of our most distinguished authors! And now you can receive a discount by ordering two or more titles!

SD#05849	MYSTERY LADY by Jackie Merritt	$2.99 ☐
SD#05867	THE BABY DOCTOR	$2.99 U.S. ☐
	by Peggy Moreland	$3.50 CAN. ☐
IM#07610	SURROGATE DAD	$3.50 U.S. ☐
	by Marion Smith Collins	$3.99 CAN. ☐
IM#07616	EYEWITNESS	$3.50 U.S. ☐
	by Kathleen Creighton	$3.99 CAN. ☐
SE#09934	THE ADVENTURER	$3.50 U.S. ☐
	by Diana Whitney	$3.99 CAN. ☐
SE#09916	AN INTERRUPTED MARRIAGE	$3.50 U.S. ☐
	by Laurey Bright	$3.99 CAN. ☐
SR#19050	MISS SCROOGE	$2.75 U.S. ☐
	by Toni Collins	$3.25 CAN. ☐
SR#08994	CALEB'S SON	$2.75 ☐
	by Laurie Paige	
YT#52001	WANTED: PERFECT PARTNER	$3.50 U.S. ☐
	by Debbie Macomber	$3.99 CAN. ☐
YT#52002	LISTEN UP, LOVER	$3.50 U.S. ☐
	by Lori Herter	$3.99 CAN. ☐

(limited quantities available on certain titles)

TOTAL AMOUNT	$_____
DEDUCT: 10% DISCOUNT FOR 2+ BOOKS	$_____
POSTAGE & HANDLING	$_____
($1.00 for one book, 50¢ for each additional)	
APPLICABLE TAXES**	$_____
TOTAL PAYABLE	$_____
(check or money order—please do not send cash)	

To order, send the completed form with your name, address, zip or postal code, along with a check or money order for the total above, payable to Silhouette Books, to: **In the U.S.:** 3010 Walden Avenue, P.O. Box 9077, Buffalo, NY 14269-9077; **In Canada:** P.O. Box 636, Fort Erie, Ontario, L2A 5X3.

Name: _____

Address: _____ City: _____

State/Prov.: _____ Zip/Postal Code: _____

**New York residents remit applicable sales taxes.
Canadian residents remit applicable GST and provincial taxes.   SBACK-MM2

Silhouette®

You're About to Become a

Privileged Woman

Reap the rewards of fabulous free gifts and benefits with proofs-of-purchase from Silhouette and Harlequin books

Pages & Privileges™

It's our way of thanking you for buying our books at your favorite retail stores.

PROOF OF PURCHASE
SD-PP115
Offer expires October 31, 1996

Harlequin and Silhouette—
the most privileged readers in the world!

For more information about Harlequin and Silhouette's PAGES & PRIVILEGES program call the Pages & Privileges Benefits Desk: 1-503-794-2499

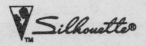

SD-PP115